"I WILL NEVER LET YOU LEAVE ME."

His lips came down on hers and swept away her fear, her unhappiness, and everything except the rapture of knowing that this was what she had been longing for and thought she had lost forever.

He kissed her while time stood still and yet she felt as she had at the cascade in the Bois, that he carried her up into the sky and they were one with the stars and no longer human but Divine.

Bantam Books by Barbara Cartland
Ask your bookseller for the books you have missed

Barbara Cartland's Library of Love Series

Dreams Do Come True

Barbara Cartland

BANTAM BOOKS
TORONTO · NEW YORK · LONDON

DREAMS DO COME TRUE

A Bantam Book / July 1981

ISBN 0-553-14750-1

Published simultaneously in the United States and Canada

Bantam Books are published by Bantam Books, Inc. Its trade-
mark, consisting of the words "Bantam Books" and the por-
trayal of a Bantam, is Registered in U.S. Patent and Trademark
Office and in other countries. Marca Registrada. Bantam
Books, Inc., 666 Fifth Avenue, New York, New York 10103.

PRINTED IN THE UNITED STATES OF AMERICA

0 9 8 7 6 5 4 3 2 1

Author's Note

Charles Frederick Worth, born in Lincolnshire, became overnight the dressmaker to the Empress Eugénie of France and the first world-wide dictator of fashion.

In the glittering, extravagant Second Empire, Worth reached the peak of international fame. He produced the crinoline as a "great novelty," then discarded it. By 1870 he employed twelve hundred seamstresses turning out hundreds of new gowns every week. His prices—sixteen hundred francs (sixty pounds) for a day-gown and one hundred pounds for an evening-gown—made people reel with shock.

But Worth turned Parisian fashion into the universal industry it is today and imitated the technique of mass production. Of all Couturiers he was the first and the greatest.

The Vedic Religion, the oldest known to have existed in India, was the starting point of Brahmanism or Hinduism. It was brought to India by the Aryans.

The Vedas were the sacred hymns and verses composed in Vedic, which is the oldest form of the Sanskrit language. No definite date can be ascribed to these compositions, many of which possess a very high literary merit, but it is believed they were written between 1500 and 1200 B.C.

Details about the British Embassy in Paris, the British Ambassador Lord Lyons and his staff are all factual.

Dreams Do
Come True

Chapter One

1869

Snowball plodded slowly down the dusty lane, moving at exactly the pace that suited him.

As he refused to hurry, whatever his rider might do, Odetta pretended she was riding a huge black stallion who would carry her with a magical swiftness over the fields to the Hall.

When they reached it there would be no Lord and Lady Walmer, but a fascinating Duke or Marquis who would invite her in to meet his friends.

They would be elegant, fashionable, amusing people who would cap each other's stories and witticisms with a sophistication that would make the conversation glitter like a constellation of stars.

This was one of Odetta's favourite day-dreams, mostly because at least two or three times a week she rode Snowball from the Vicarage to the Hall.

It was no use resenting the time it took because he was old. It was easier to imagine him as a spirited Thoroughbred with Arab blood, which she could see so clearly in her mind that she believed he really existed.

They reached the impressive iron gates set between two stone lodges, and now Snowball could have moved a little more swiftly across the Park under the trees, rather than keep to the gravel drive.

But while Odetta preferred the grassland, Snowball was quite happy to take the direct route to the Hall because he knew it would bring him sooner to the comfortable stables where he would wait for his mistress.

Odetta was sure he calculated that the hay and the oats with which he was provided at the Hall were of better quality than those he was given at home.

Giving up the struggle to coax him onto the grass, Odetta stared ahead to the Hall, which looked extremely impressive with its grey stone touched with gold by the sun and Lord Walmer's personal standard flying above the roof.

However, it was not her dream-house, which was very much larger and built by the famous Robert Adam, rather than the obscure architect who was responsible for the erection of the Hall at the beginning of the century.

Nevertheless, Odetta thought, after the simplicity of the small Vicarage, the Walmers' home was, by contrast, extremely grand.

"If I had money," she told herself, "I would redecorate the Drawing-Room in silver and gold, and have a deep Madonna-blue carpet up the staircase to replace the patterned one in that rather ugly shade of red."

She always found it fascinating to imagine how she would change and improve other people's houses.

Just as when she looked at other women, whether old or young, she had an immediate mental picture of how she would improve their appearance by re-dressing them.

However, one person whose appearance she would not alter was Lady Walmer.

She was actually wondering which of her many gowns Lady Walmer would be wearing this afternoon when Snowball reached the front door.

Odetta dismounted, and as she did so, a stable-boy who must have been waiting for her came to Snowball's head, touching his forelock as he said:

" 'Afternoon, Miss!"

"Good-afternoon, Joe! Is Miss Penelope indoors?"

"Her be that, Miss," Joe said, and without wasting any more time in conversation he led Snowball off towards the stables.

Odetta ran up the steps.

The door was open and it did not surprise her that there was nobody in the Hall.

She expected that Bateman, the Butler, was still busy clearing away the luncheon.

But there was no need for her to be announced or for anyone to be told that she had arrived.

She knew her way up the stairs to the Sitting-Room on the First Floor, which had once been the School-Room, and now, since Penelope had grown up, was elevated into being called a "Sitting-Room."

She opened the door, and as she expected Penelope was there waiting for her, looking rather thick-set and lumpy in a gown that Odetta had never liked.

It was not only the wrong colour for Penelope's dark hair and rather sallow complexion, but it also made her waist look thicker than it actually was and accentuated the fact that she was too short and too fat for the present fashions.

To Penelope, all that mattered at the moment was that Odetta had arrived, and as the Sitting-Room door opened, she jumped up with a little cry to exclaim:

"I have been watching for you! You must have arrived while I was still downstairs."

"You know how slow Snowball is," Odetta said with a smile.

"But you are here!" Penelope said. "I have something awful to tell you."

Odetta looked surprised.

She had been at the Hall only yesterday, and nothing untoward had occurred then.

"What is it?" she enquired.

"We are going to Paris!"

"To Paris?" Odetta exclaimed. "How exciting. But why?"

"The Prime Minister has asked Papa to attend some Conference or other, and Step-Mama and I are to go with him."

"It is the most thrilling thing I have ever heard!" Odetta said. "How lucky you are!"

To her surprise, Penelope turned her head away and said gloomily:

"I have no wish to go."

"No wish to go?" Odetta echoed. "Can you really be saying such a thing?"

Penelope glanced towards the door to see that it was closed. Then she moved towards the window-seat, saying:

"Come and sit down beside me. I have something to tell you."

The way she spoke surprised Odetta, but she obeyed, moving with a grace which her friend Penelope sadly lacked, and sat down sideways on the soft cushion on the window-seat.

As she did so, she pulled off her plain straw bonnet and the sunshine touching the gold of her hair seemed to make it spring into life.

There was a great difference between the girls, for unlike Penelope Walmer, Odetta Charlwood was very slender and much taller than her friend, with a sweet expression on her face that was very much in keeping with her character.

The starriness of her grey eyes revealed that she lived half the time in a world of make-believe. But there were dimples on either side of her mouth, which, when she was laughing, gave her face an almost mischievous look which was very attractive.

But both her eyes and her voice were serious as she asked:

"What are you keeping from me, Penelope? I cannot believe that you really do not wish to visit Paris."

Again Penelope glanced over her shoulder as if she was terrified of being overheard. Then she said:

"I was going to tell you . . . sooner or . . . later, Odetta . . . that I am in . . . love!"

Odetta stared at her in astonishment before she asked:

"In love? But with whom?"

As she spoke, her mind searched frantically among the men who came to the Hall for one on whom Penelope was likely to bestow her heart.

Of course the Walmers entertained generously, for Lady Walmer was very fashionable and liked to spend as much time in London as her husband would allow. But her friends were invariably married, like herself.

Because Odetta spent a great deal of time at the Hall, she did not miss the fact that there was a stream of elegant gentlemen paying court to Penelope's Stepmother, but none of them had shown the slightest interest in Penelope, nor, as far as she knew, were any of them bachelors.

Of course she was far too kind and too tactful even to hint at it, but she had in fact been very worried about Penelope now that she was grown up and was still living at home.

Her Stepmother was infinitely more attractive than she was, and Lady Walmer made it obvious that she resented the fact that she had to chaperone her husband's daughter.

Unfortunately, Penelope did not resemble her mother, who had died two years ago, but took after her father.

Lord Walmer, dark, heavily built, and over six feet

tall, was quite a good-looking man, but his features on a woman were not prepossessing, nor was his daughter's rather thick-set figure conducive to elegance.

Yet Odetta knew that Penelope had a kind disposition, a loving heart for those on whom she bestowed her affection, and a loyalty which was one of her most sterling qualities.

However, she was shy and reserved, perhaps because she had no mother to guide and help her, and she clung to Odetta, who like herself was motherless, although she had no Stepmother to make her life difficult in a hundred different ways.

"Who is it? With whom can you be in love?" Odetta asked as Penelope did not speak.

In a voice that was barely above a whisper, Penelope replied:

"It is . . . Simon Johnson . . . and he . . . loves me, Odetta. He . . . told me so yesterday."

Odetta was astonished, as well she might be.

Simon Johnson was the younger son of a yeoman Squire who lived on the other side of the little village of Edenham.

She had known him all her life and had always thought him a dull, over-serious young man. That Penelope should love him, and he her, was so astonishing that for the moment Odetta could think of nothing to say.

"But where have you met . . . and how did you know him . . . well enough?" she managed to ask after a long pause.

As she spoke, she was thinking that neither Squire Johnson nor his sons were ever invited to the Hall, except for a meet of the foxhounds or when a point-to-point took place on Lord Walmer's Estate.

"It all . . . happened a month . . . ago," Penelope said a little breathlessly. "I was riding in the morning with Sam when his horse went lame."

Sam was one of the grooms who usually accompanied Penelope when she went riding.

"Sam walked his horse back to the stables," Penelope went on, "and I went on alone."

She paused to draw in her breath, and her rather plain face became quite pretty as she said:

"I met . . . Simon as he was bringing a note from his father . . . and we talked, and he . . . told me about a litter of puppies which his spaniel had just had."

Odetta was listening intently and Penelope continued:

"He said he wanted to show them to me, and of course I wanted to see them, but I knew there would be a fuss if I asked Papa if I could visit the Johnsons."

"So what did you do?" Odetta asked, knowing the answer.

"Simon said he would bring a gig and collect me if I would walk to the edge of the Home-Wood."

Odetta listened with astonishment. It was so unlike Penelope to take the initiative or to do anything that was not completely conformable.

"So you went alone?"

"I said I had a headache and was going to lie down after tea," Penelope replied.

Odetta thought this was quite a clever idea on her part, because if her Stepmother had guests she usually did not want Penelope there, while if the family was alone, Lady Walmer would lie down until dinner-time so as to look her best, especially if there was to be a party.

"So you saw the puppies?" Odetta prompted.

"As a matter of fact I did not," Penelope answered. "We drove through the woods where no-one was likely to see us, and Simon said he thought it was a mistake after all for me to go to his house, in case his father and mother talked and Papa heard I had been there."

"Your father would certainly have thought it wrong for you to go alone with him," Odetta observed.

"Yes, I know," Penelope agreed, "but when Simon told

me what he felt about me, I knew I had to be very clever if I wished to go on seeing him—which I did."

"What did he feel about you?" Odetta asked curiously.

Penelope's eyes lit up.

"He said he had always admired me when he had seen me out hunting, and wanted to know me. Then last night, when we met for the sixth or seventh time, I cannot remember which, he said he—loved me."

"That was very quick," Odetta said.

Penelope shook her head.

"Not really," she answered. "We have been living near to each other for eighteen years, and now when I look back I know I was always—conscious of him whenever I saw him. Once I asked Papa if we could have the Johnson boys to a party."

"What did he answer?" Odetta asked.

"He paused for a moment," Penelope replied, "then he said: 'Squire Johnson is a decent man and I respect him, but socially, Penelope, they are not in our class.' "

Odetta gave a little sigh because this was what she would have expected Lord Walmer to say, but before she could reply, Penelope said in a pleading voice:

"Odetta, what am I to—do? I—love him, and I want to—marry him!"

There was an appeal in Penelope's voice which Odetta did not miss, and instinctively she put out her hands to take those of her friend.

"It is going to be difficult, Penelope dear."

"I know," Penelope agreed, "but however much Papa may want me to make a brilliant social marriage, I swear I will not marry . . . anybody but . . . Simon!"

Odetta looked worried.

She knew that Lord Walmer was rich, and Penelope was his only child. Of course he would want her to marry somebody who was socially acceptable and of whom he

approved, and she knew as well as Penelope did that
Simon was not in that category.

Because she thought it was something she ought to
say, she held Penelope's hands very tightly and asked:

"You do not think, dearest, it would be wisest to try to
forget Simon? And perhaps that is what you will do in
Paris."

"I shall never forget him if I meet a million men!"
Penelope replied positively. "I know he is the right person for me. just as he says I am the right person for him.
It is not something we can explain in—words, it is just
something we both—feel."

"That is what you should feel for the man you marry,"
Odetta said almost beneath her breath.

"I knew you would understand," Penelope said. "In
the stories you have told me ever since we were small,
true love always conquers in the end and the Prince finds
the girl he really wanted to marry, even if she is poor and
ragged."

Her voice was deep with feeling as she added:

"What I feel for Simon is one of your fairy-stories
come true, Odetta."

"Oh, dearest, I do want you to be happy," Odetta
cried, "but you know how difficult your father is going to
be about this."

Penelope's eyes darkened.

"Yes, I know, and Simon says it would be a mistake to
tell him now. We just have to wait, and if it is impossible
for us to be married with Papa's blessing, then we shall
have to run away."

"Run away?" Odetta echoed.

Penelope nodded.

"We would hide until we could get married somehow.
Then perhaps I will—have a—baby, and it will be too
late for Papa to separate us."

Odetta was astonished, not only that Penelope should talk in such a way but that she should have thought it all out.

She had always seemed a rather unimaginative, simple person, and Odetta had been the leader, the guide, and the inspiration not only in every game they had played but in everything they had thought since they had been children.

Because there were few families in the rather isolated countryside of South Lincolnshire, Penelope and Odetta, being of the same age, had played together when they were both in their prams and had been close friends ever since.

The first Lady Walmer had been fond of Odetta's mother, and it had been a sensible arrangement for their daughters to share a Governess.

In summer or winter, in rain or fine weather, Odetta had found her way from the Vicarage to the Hall, where Penelope and their Governess would be waiting for her in the School-Room.

When Lady Walmer had died and a year later Lord Walmer had married again, things had changed.

The new Lady Walmer had made it quite clear that she was not impressed by the Vicar, whom she found a bore, nor by his daughter.

"Surely there are more congenial friends with whom Penelope can spend her time than that girl from the Vicarage?" she had said to her husband.

"Odetta is a nice little thing," Lord Walmer replied, "and Penelope is fond of her."

"That is as may be," Lady Walmer said sharply, "but Penelope is coming out next season, and the sooner we start finding an eligible husband for her, the better."

"There is no hurry," Lord Walmer replied.

"On the contrary, the sooner a girl is married, the better," his wife answered, "and quite frankly, I find a *ménage à trois* a bore. I would much rather be alone with—you."

Lord Walmer appreciated his wife's flattery, and since he was not a very perceptive man it did not strike him that she deeply resented having to chaperone a girl when she considered herself still a young woman.

But Lady Walmer had made up her mind that the quickest way of ridding herself of the encumbrance was to get Penelope married off and therefore out of the house.

The difficulty, of course, was Penelope herself.

No-one appreciated better than Lady Walmer that Penelope was plain, dull, and not rich enough to be attractive to the fortune-hunters.

However, she had done her best by taking Penelope to London and having her fitted out by the most expensive dressmakers in Bond Street.

She then arranged some dinner-parties at Lord Walmer's house in Berkeley Square, and also took Penelope to a number of Balls, where she stood most of the evening beside one of the Dowagers, while Lady Walmer danced every dance and had more partners than she could possibly accept.

"It was ghastly!" Penelope told Odetta when they returned to the country. "I hated every minute of it, and if I have to do it again, I swear I will drown myself in the lake!"

Odetta, who had been left behind, could not help feeling a little wistfully that she would have liked the opportunity to see London and attend at least one of the Balls which Penelope had found so unpleasant.

She had often told herself stories of how the ladies with their huge crinolines swinging round the Ball-rooms under the chandeliers would look like swans.

She could visualise the grace of their movements, the glitter of the jewels on their heads and round their necks, and the elegance of the handsome men with whom they danced.

Penelope's version of what occurred was not in the least like Odetta's day-dreams, and what was more, Odetta thought that her friend's gowns were by no means as attractive or as flattering as they could be.

She was not quite certain what was wrong, but she knew that instead of improving Penelope's appearance they contrived to accentuate her bad points and neglect the good ones.

Looking at her friend dispassionately, Odetta knew she had pretty eyes that shone with a sincerity that any observant man would find attractive.

Her skin was clear and white, but because she was short, a crinoline made her look more dumpy and unattractive than she actually was.

Then Odetta asked herself what the alternative was. Everybody wore a crinoline!

Although hers was a small one and she kept it for special occasions, she and Hannah, who had helped her make her gowns ever since she could remember, had contrived by adding dozens of stiff petticoats to make her simple muslin dresses seem as full as the fashion decreed.

She was fortunate in that her waist was tiny, and although she did not realise it, everything she wore seemed to add to the elusive, fairy-like quality of her appearance, which was echoed by the stories that came into her mind.

Now, because it was a tale of love and she knew that it had brought something magical into Penelope's life that had never been there before, she said impulsively:

"I understand what you are feeling, dearest, and I will help you . . . you know I will . . . if you want me to, but it is going to be difficult . . . very, very difficult to convince your father that you should marry Simon Johnson."

"He will never agree," Penelope said simply, "and although Simon says we must not do anything too quickly, I know that sooner or later we shall have to brave

Papa's wrath and either tell him that I intend to marry Simon, or else inform him that I am already married when it is too late for him to do anything about it."

Then she gave a cry that was like the sound of a small animal.

"Now you . . . understand why I cannot go to . . . Paris."

"But you will have to go."

"Perhaps Simon will be able to—prevent it."

Odetta thought this was unlikely, and she asked:

"When are you meeting him?"

Penelope looked at the clock.

"In half-an-hour."

"Half-an-hour?" Odetta echoed. "Where?"

"In the usual place at the end of the wood. That is why I sent a groom with a note for you as soon as Papa said at breakfast this morning that we were going to Paris. I know how clever you are, Odetta, and I am sure you can think of some way I can stay at home."

"You want me to come with you and talk to Simon?"

"Of course," Penelope answered. "I meant to tell you about him yesterday, but, if you remember, Step-mama kept coming in and out of the room and I was terrified in case she should overhear what we were saying."

"It would be wise not to let her know anything at the moment."

"She wants me to get married," Penelope said, "so as to get me out of her way, but I am quite certain she will think that the Johnsons are beneath her condescension."

Odetta knew that this was true.

"I know I shall like them," Penelope said fiercely, "and I should be miserable if I had to marry one of the men I met in London. I cannot tell you, Odetta, how horrible they were. Blasé, selfish, and indifferent to anything except their own interests."

Odetta had heard this before, but she knew that because Penelope had been a wallflower at the Balls and over-shadowed by her Stepmother, she had a very jaundiced idea of London Society.

At the same time, she was astute enough to realise that whatever she might feel, her father still would not accept a man like Simon Johnson as an eligible suitor.

Before she could speak, Penelope sprang to her feet.

"Come on, let us start walking through the woods," she said. "No-one will suspect us of doing anything unusual, and I know Step-mama is expecting a lot of boring people to tea."

"In which case she will not want me here," Odetta said quickly.

"No, of course not!" Penelope cried. "And I have already told the servants that we will have tea upstairs. If she does not want you, she will not want me either!"

Odetta had seen some of Lady Walmer's friends. Most of them were not living in the County but staying with those few of the neighbours whom she thought interesting.

Odetta could understand how Penelope felt out-of-place amongst them.

Lady Walmer had always been acclaimed as a beauty. When she was very young she had been married to a man who both drank and gambled.

He had been conveniently killed in a Steeple-Chase, leaving his wife penniless and with no other assets except her beauty.

It had been a Godsend when Lord Walmer, recently bereaved and lonely as a man can be after a long and happy marriage, sat next to her at a dinner-party and fell for the allurements which she could, when she wished, use extremely effectively.

They were married within two months, and Penelope found herself with a Stepmother who was very different in every way from what her mother had been.

Lady Walmer made no pretence about disliking the

country and wishing to spend as much time as possible in London.

But Lord Walmer was very conscious of his duty to his Estates, and, despite every enticement his wife used, he insisted on staying for months at the Hall.

Odetta was sure that the one person who would be thrilled at the idea of going to Paris would be Lady Walmer, and this was confirmed when as the two girls were walking down the stairs, ostensibly to start out on their walk in the garden, they met Her Ladyship in the Hall.

"Good-afternoon!" she said coldly as Odetta curtseyed to her. "I thought you were here with us yesterday?"

"Yes, Ma'am, I was," Odetta answered.

"Well, you will miss Penelope when she goes to Paris," Lady Walmer said. "I suppose she has told you how excited we all are at the prospect?"

"Yes, indeed, Ma'am," Odetta replied, "and I can imagine nothing more thrilling than to visit Paris and see all the improvements that have been made to the city."

Lady Walmer laughed scornfully.

"It is not the improvements in which I am interested," she said, "but the chance to visit *Monsieur* Worth, and have some decent clothes for once. Do you know that the crinoline is now completely out-of-date, and he has introduced a new fashion which has not yet reached London?"

Because she was talking on a subject that really interested her, Lady Walmer not only was animated but was speaking to Odetta quite pleasantly, which was unusual.

"The crinoline is out-of-date?" Odetta exclaimed. "How extraordinary!"

"That is what Worth has decreed, and the first thing I shall do when we reach Paris is to buy dozens and dozens of new gowns."

"It will be interesting for you not only to see the gowns but to meet Mr. Worth himself," Odetta said. "As you know, Ma'am, he was born in Bourne."

As she spoke, she expected Lady Walmer to be aware of this, but now she looked at Odetta in astonishment and said:

"In Bourne? How do you know this?"

"Everybody knows that round here," Odetta said. "His father lived in North Street, and he was christened in the Abbey Church."

"I did not know it," Lady Walmer said, "but when I reach Paris I shall certainly tell him that I like his hometown."

Odetta had the idea that Lady Walmer was glad of this opportunity to attract the attenton of the great man.

No-one could live in this part of Lincolnshire without being aware that Charles Worth, whose father had been a Solicitor in the nearby village of Hodlingham, had by now retrieved the family name after his father became bankrupt and deserted his wife and children.

The story of Charles Worth's success was common gossip not only in the town but in all the nearby villages, and for the last few years people seldom came to see Odetta's father and mother without talking of the success of young Worth in becoming the first male dressmaker in the world.

A great number of the older ladies were shocked at the whole idea.

"I call it immodest, that is what I call it!" one of them said to her mother in Odetta's hearing, when stories filtered back to Bourne of the gorgeous gowns he personally fitted on the Empress Eugénie and the other beautiful women of Paris.

"It is certainly unusual," Mrs. Charlwood had said gently.

"They say he charges as much as one hundred pounds for a dress, Mrs. Charlwood—think of that! It is a scandal for any woman, even an Empress, to spend so much money on clothes!"

Her mother had been inclined to agree, but the tales of the lovely and imaginative gowns that Worth designed for the French ladies fired Odetta's imagination.

As she grew older, the heroines of her stories, the Cinderellas who became Princesses, all wore Worth gowns of the glamorous fabrics which the inhabitants of Bourne had learnt that he favoured.

Tulle, silk, satin, and brocade were recited almost like words in a poem, and Odetta knew that the local ladies for the first time looked critically at their moires, grosgrains, velvets, and heavy wools.

Charles Worth seemed to creep into the conversation if anyone was buying eggs in the market-place or a few yards of ribbon at the haberdashers.

It was not surprising that he caught the public fancy, for nothing sensational ever happened in Bourne.

It was a quiet, sleepy little town with nothing particular to recommend it except a Mill and the Abbey Church of St. Peter's and St. Paul's, where Worth had been christened.

The people who lived in Bourne had mostly for generations followed the trade of their parents and grandparents.

To Odetta, Worth's success was just like one of the stories that she made up for herself.

In the very beginning, after his father had deserted his family and young Charles Frederick's mother had found work as a Housekeeper, it must have been fate that had made her decide that her son should go to work for a London Draper.

All the ladies in Bourne were aware that he raised his fare to London by making Easter bonnets for them! Odetta had tried to find out what they looked like, but no-one could tell her.

What was told and retold was that he had reached London, found a job as an apprentice in Swan and Edgar's, and for years, after working in the shop all day, at night he would sleep under the counter.

Odetta worried over his sufferings and privations, because somehow she felt almost hurt at the thought of all he had had to do when he was so young.

She liked to speak of the time when he decided to go to Paris because all the best materials came from France.

Although he had saved every penny he could from his meagre wages and had gone hungry to do so, he still had not enough to pay his fare, and his mother had had to beg the money from her relatives.

Then, on his twentieth birthday, in the winter of 1845, Charles Frederick Worth had caught the steamer from London Bridge, starting off on an adventure which Odetta felt must have been as thrilling as the moment when Jason set off in search of the Golden Fleece.

Thinking of Worth and all she knew about him, she had for a moment slipped away from reality, and now she heard Lady Walmer say with a sharp note in her voice:

"Are you really telling me the truth, Odetta, about Charles Worth? It is not another of those fairy-stories which you have invented? For in that case I shall be extremely annoyed."

"No, indeed, it is the truth," Odetta insisted, "as anyone in Bourne will tell you."

"I have no intention of talking to the people in Bourne about Worth," Lady Walmer replied, "but you can tell me about his childhood, because I want to know about him."

As she spoke, Odetta felt that her first impression had been right and Lady Walmer wished to ingratiate herself with the great Couturier.

It struck her for a moment that it was almost amusing that Lady Walmer, who thought herself so beautiful and so smart and who was indeed a person of consequence in

London, should be eager to please a man who in her estimation was nothing more than a tradesman.

But Odetta knew that all the tales about him were true and he was in fact something very much more than that.

Because she was so used to hearing about him, he had become as familiar to her as were the Walmers, the Johnsons, the Vicar of Bourne, and even her own father.

Although she had never met Charles Worth, she thought of him as being part of her life.

Now it was quite a shock to find someone living at the Hall who knew nothing about him except that he was the greatest designer of gowns in the world, and that not only the French Empress but the Queen of every Court in Europe were his customers.

Meanwhile, Lady Walmer was waiting to hear about him, and as Odetta gave her a smile, she realised that Penelope was also looking at her insistently.

"I want the truth, Odetta!" Lady Walmer said. "I do not want to hear a lot of your make-believe stories! While I do not say they are lies, you certainly exaggerate the truth and often distort it! So be careful what you tell me, or I shall be extremely annoyed!"

For a moment Odetta's dimples appeared in her cheeks and changed her expression. Then she said humbly:

"It is rather difficult to sift the exaggerations, as you call them, Ma'am, from the truth, but I will try to give you the facts as I know them, because I have always felt that Mr. Worth is a very special and unique person."

"That is exactly what he is," Lady Walmer agreed, "and his gowns are fantastic! Quite, quite fantastic! What I buy in Paris will be quite different from anything I have ever bought before."

"You will look very lovely in them," Odetta said.

She was not paying a compliment, she was merely stating a fact, and Lady Walmer gave her a smile which was for the first time quite friendly.

"I am going to try to dazzle Paris," she said, "and the only person who can make me able to do that is Charles Worth, so hurry and tell me all about him. You had better come into the Drawing-Room."

Lady Walmer walked across the Hall as she spoke, and as Odetta started to follow her, she was aware that Penelope gave her a despairing glance.

She knew that she was longing to start off for the woods where Simon Johnson would be waiting.

But Odetta knew not only that she must do what Lady Walmer asked, but that at the same time it might be a good idea from Penelope's point of view to put her in a good temper.

She therefore gave Penelope a reassuring smile, and with a movement of her lips she hinted that she would not be long.

Then she entered the Drawing-Room, where she knew Lady Walmer was waiting impatiently to hear what she had to say.

Chapter Two

"It is not true, I am dreaming!" Odetta told herself as the train started off for Calais and she tried to realise that she actually was in France.

It seemed so incredible that she was quite certain she was living in one of her day-dreams and it was going on longer than usual.

When she had said to her father: "I am going up to the Hall to say good-bye to Penelope, who is going to Paris," he had not answered.

This did not surprise Odetta, because like herself he was very vague when he was concentrating on something else.

At the moment, the Reverend Arthur Charlwood was working on a book which was occupying him to the point where he was barely conscious of what was going on in the world round him.

It was to be a volume on the influence of Greek thought on Christianity, and although he had already filled three manuscript-books, he was only halfway through it.

This book, like his last—*The Influence of the Vedas on Civilisation*—would undoubtedly be praised by scholars but would arouse little interest amongst the general public.

Since his wife's death, the Reverend Arthur had become more and more absorbed in his work, and if Odetta and Hannah had not reminded him continually, he would never have remembered the Church Services he had to give and certainly not the weddings and funerals.

"Did you hear what I said, Papa?" Odetta asked. "Penelope and her parents are going to Paris."

Her voice was insistent, and her father raised his head from the book which he was reading while he ate his breakfast.

"What did you say—Paris? An interesting city. I remember . . ."

He was just about to indulge in a long reminiscence about the time he had spent in Paris as a young man, when Odetta interrupted him.

"Lord Walmer has been asked by the Prime Minister to visit Paris for a Conference, Papa, and they are all to stay at the British Embassy."

Now her father was really interested.

"The Embassy!" he exclaimed. "Now, that was bought by the Duke of Wellington from the Princess Paulina Borghese, and I remember that when I dined there many years ago I thought it a very interesting building. I understood Wellington's desire to make it a British property."

Odetta had given a little sigh.

It was impossible to make her father as interested in the present as he was in the past.

She wanted somebody to share with her the excitement she felt over Penelope's visit to France, even though Penelope herself became more and more depressed about it every day that passed.

Odetta could understand her reluctance to leave Simon after she had seen the two of them together.

She had suspected that Penelope was exaggerating in saying that Simon Johnson was in love with her, but now she realised that her friend had spoken no less than the truth.

Simon obviously both admired and loved Penelope in the same way that she loved him.

Although they had talked for a long time on the edge of the woods, they had none of them come to any conclusion as to how they could approach Lord Walmer.

Meanwhile, both Odetta and Simon were faced with the task of persuading Penelope that the only thing she could do was to visit France with her father.

"If you make up your mind to refuse to go, you will have to offer a very convincing reason," Odetta said after a lot of discussion. "For if your father suspects that you want to stay behind to be with Simon, it will make him absolutely determined that it is the one thing you should not do."

Finally Penelope agreed that she would go to Paris, but she said to Simon desperately:

"I shall be counting every hour, every minute, every second, until I can return and see you again."

"I shall be doing the same," he replied.

Then as they looked into each other's eyes, there was no need for words to tell Odetta how much they resented the thought of being parted.

"Now that you have seen Simon, you know what I . . . feel," Penelope said as they walked back through the woods.

"I do understand," Odetta said in a soft voice, "but for the moment I cannot think what you can do about it."

"You must pray—you must pray very hard, Odetta, for Simon and me to be together," Penelope pleaded. "After all, you are a Parson's daughter and God ought to listen to you!"

"You make it sound as if I had some special influence with Him," Odetta said with a smile. "But I think, Penelope dearest, your prayers will be just as effective as mine."

"I have prayed and prayed," Penelope answered, "but so far the only solution I can think of is that Simon and I must run away."

"I am sure that would make your father very angry."

"Of course he will be angry!" Penelope agreed, "but he would be just as angry if I asked his permission to marry Simon! However, if we do run away, there is going to be the problem of where we can live, and what money we shall have."

"I suppose Simon has very little," Odetta said, knowing he was the younger son.

"Just the allowance his father gives him, and I have the same," Penelope said. "But I would live in a cave or a wood-cutter's hut with him and be happy."

Odetta knew she was speaking the truth, but it still did not make things any easier.

When they parted, Penelope said:

"Come and say good-bye to me tomorrow, and as there will be no chance of my seeing Simon again, I will give you a letter for him."

"Very well," Odetta agreed.

As usual, Snowball took an unconscionable time reaching the Hall the next day.

Odetta knew the Walmers were having an early luncheon and leaving on the afternoon train to London, where they were to stay the night before leaving from Victoria Station the following morning.

As her father always breakfasted early so that he could get on with his book before he was interrupted by parochial matters, Odetta actually arrived at the Hall well before nine o'clock.

As usual, a groom took Snowball away to the stables, and she ran up the stairs, expecting to find Penelope in her bedroom.

She was there, but so was Lady Walmer, looking extremely attractive in an elaborate negligee of silk and

lace, with her hair covered by a coquettish lace cap
ornamented with bows of satin ribbon.

As Odetta walked into the room without knocking it
was obvious that there was trouble, and she heard Lady
Walmer say in a most disagreeable voice:

"If you think you are going to share Emelene with me,
you are much mistaken! She has quite enough to do
looking after my clothes, especially with all the new gowns
I shall buy."

"Then whom shall I take?" Penelope asked.

Lady Walmer was just about to make some tart reply,
when she turned her head and saw Odetta in the doorway.

"So you are here again!" she said. "Perhaps you can
decide whom Penelope can take with her to Paris as a
lady's-maid?"

"A lady's-maid?" Odetta questioned. "What has happened
to Martha?"

Martha had been Penelope's lady's-maid ever since
Lord Walmer had dispensed with a Nanny and handed
Penelope over to a Governess.

Martha had been one of the housemaids, and Penelope's
mother, knowing how attached she was to her daughter,
had promoted Martha to look after Penelope, which she
did with competence and affection.

"Martha fell down the stairs last night," Penelope said
before her Stepmother could speak. "The Doctor says
she has fractured a bone in her leg and will not be able to
walk for at least three weeks."

"So now you see our problem," Lady Walmer added
sourly. "I have told Penelope she will have to take one of
the housemaids with her."

"You know how hopeless they are at packing," Penelope
answered, "and Martha has always said that they press
gowns abominably, so she has never let them touch any
of my things."

Odetta knew this was true.

The housemaids were all girls from the village, and although they would have been willing to learn to do things for Penelope, Martha was very possessive and had never allowed them to wash and press so much as a handkerchief.

Odetta racked her brains as to whom she could suggest, for she knew everyone in the Walmer household and was aware that they were all unsuitable in any positions except the ones they occupied already. Therefore, she made no reply.

"We are being very stupid!" Penelope exclaimed suddenly. "If I have to go to Paris, Odetta must come with me!"

Not only Odetta but Lady Walmer stared at her in astonishment as she went on:

"Odetta sews like an angel, Step-Mama, and she makes all her own gowns. It would be lovely to have her with me, and we can do things together when you want to be with your friends."

As Odetta, stupefied by the idea, looked at Penelope, she was aware that Lady Walmer was assimilating what her Stepdaughter had said and thinking how it could benefit herself.

Then she said slowly, as if she weighed every word:

"I—suppose—that is a—possibility."

"Of course it is!" Penelope said quickly. "If I have to buy clothes as Papa says I have to, then Odetta can come with me for the fittings, as I am sure, Step-Mama, you will be too busy to do so."

Odetta thought that tipped the balance in her favour, and Lady Walmer said:

"Very well. As there appears to be no alternative, we will take Odetta, but let me make one thing clear."

She looked at Odetta as she spoke, her eyes taking in the girl's appearance, and Odetta felt she was not pleased with what she saw.

"If we take you," she said, "you will come just as a maid—a companion to Penelope—and nothing else. You will not eat with us except when we are alone, and you will not accompany us to any of the places to which we are invited."

"Of course, Ma'am, I understand," Odetta said quickly. "It would be a very great privilege indeed to come with you to Paris. I will try to make myself useful and not get in your way."

"If you do, I shall send you back!" Lady Walmer snapped.

She looked at her Stepdaughter with an expression in her eyes which Odetta knew was one of dislike.

"As for you, Penelope," she said, "you can consider yourself a very lucky girl, not only in being taken to Paris with your father and me, but in that he has promised you two Worth gowns, so that you will be one of the privileged women who have been dressed by Worth."

Odetta knew by the way she spoke that Lady Walmer was annoyed that her Stepdaughter was to have Worth gowns, for she considered them to be her perquisite alone.

Lady Walmer did not wait for Penelope's answer. She merely swept from the bedroom, saying as she passed Odetta:

"I suppose the brake which is taking the luggage and Emelene to the station had better pick you up. If you are not ready, you will be left behind."

The door shut behind her, and Odetta gave a little gasp.

"Did she . . . really say I could . . . come with you to . . . Paris?" she asked in a voice which did not sound like her own.

"She did, and it will make things a little better for me," Penelope answered. "At least I can talk to you about Simon."

*   *   *

In the rush that followed—getting back to the Vicarage, helping Hannah to pack her clothes, telling her father she was leaving, and being ready in time for the brake which was carrying the luggage, Emelene, and Lord Walmer's valet—Odetta had no time to think.

Everything seemed unreal except that it was wildly exciting to stay the night in London, to travel by train to Dover, and to cross the Channel in one of the new paddle-steamers.

Now she was actually in France, and because they were alone in the compartment, Penelope was talking interminably about Simon.

But Odetta was looking out the windows at the hedgeless fields stretching away towards the horizon, the white bullocks, the roads lined with high trees on either side of them, and finding it a fascination that was difficult to translate into words.

"Oh, Odetta, I love him so much!" Penelope was saying. "How long do you think it will be before I see him again?"

It was a question that Penelope had already asked a hundred times, but there was no answer, because Lord Walmer had no idea how long he would be obliged to stay in France.

Although she thought it was a little disloyal to Penelope, Odetta could not help hoping that what he had to do would not be finished too quickly.

There was so much she wished to see, so much she wanted to learn!

They arrived in Paris at eight o'clock in the evening, and there were two smart carriages at the station waiting to carry them to the Embassy.

It had been difficult to have a chance to talk to Lord Walmer, but Odetta had managed it when she and Penelope moved from the compartment they were occupying to join her parents for a meal.

"Will you tell me about the Ambassador, My Lord?"
Odetta asked pleadingly. "When Papa visited the Embassy, the Marquis of Normanby was Ambassador, so he
has never met Lord Lyons."

Lord Walmer smiled.

"Your father must have been there a long time ago."

Odetta nodded.

"I think he was quite a young man. Has the present
Ambassador been there long?"

"No, indeed. He was only appointed two years ago,"
Lord Walmer replied, "and he was in Washington before
that."

"Is he very clever?" Odetta enquired.

"I believe so, but he is in fact a shy man, and those
who want to disparage him say that he looks like a country Squire."

This remark made Odetta think of Simon and that it
was a pity that his father was not an Ambassador.

She learnt as the day progressed that Lord Lyons was
a bachelor and was more attached to his Manchester
terrier, who was called "Toby," than to anyone else.

But Lord Walmer told her very little more, and when
they finally arrived at the Embassy and Lord Lyons appeared
to greet them, she found that he was a very large, shy
man, inclined to be silent and, from what she learnt
later, over-cautious.

They met Mr. George Sheffield, who ran the house and
was very obliging, as was Mr. Edward Malet, who was
the Ambassador's Secretary.

They were all very tired and even Odetta felt glad to
undress and get into bed.

Her room was next to Penelope's and when they bade
each other good-night Odetta said:

"I can never be sufficiently grateful to you, dearest
Penelope, for bringing me here. I used sometimes to

dream that I should visit Paris, and now that it has actually happened, it is more exciting than anything I could imagine. Thank you, thank you!"

"I should feel like that too if I were with Simon," Penelope said in a low voice.

"I think Simon would want you to enjoy yourself."

"You do not think he will forget me?"

It was a cry of fear, and Odetta said quickly:

"Of course he will not! When he has loved you for so long, he will hardly be likely to change because you are away from him for a few weeks."

"No, of course not, and I will write to him every day," Penelope said, "and you can post the letters for me so that there is no chance of Step-Mama seeing them and asking questions."

"Of course I will," Odetta promised. "Good-night, dearest."

She slept almost as soon as her head touched the pillow, but she awoke early in the morning and stood at the window looking out onto the garden at the back of the house.

With its well-arranged formal flower-beds and high trees, it was very unlike what she had expected to find in a town.

But Odetta felt that everything in Paris would be unexpected and, she was quite certain, beautiful.

She was dressed long before Penelope even awoke, then after they had breakfast with Lord Walmer because Lady Walmer never appeared until much later in the day, Odetta asked eagerly:

"What shall we do? Do you think we could explore some of Paris?"

"I suppose we shall have to ask Step-Mama first," Penelope replied.

"Yes, of course," Odetta agreed, "and you had better do so. I have a feeling I had better keep out of sight and make myself as unobtrusive as possible."

Because Penelope knew this was wise, she did not argue.

She went upstairs, and when she came down again she said:

"We are to wait until Step-Mama is ready. Then we are to go shopping."

Odetta's eyes lit up.

She was quite certain from what had been said on the journey that the one shop that Lady Walmer intended to visit before any of the others was situated at No. 7 Rue de la Paix.

She was not mistaken, and two hours later, when Penelope had had time to write several pages of a letter to Simon, with Odetta "keeping cave" in case her Step-mother appeared unexpectedly and questioned her as to what she was doing, Lady Walmer came into the Salon.

She was dressed in one of her smartest and most elaborate London gowns and had applied more cosmetics than usual. But as they drove away from the Embassy in the open carriage which was waiting for them, Odetta had the strange idea that she was nervous.

"Tell me more about *Monsieur* Worth's family," Lady Walmer said to Odetta. "Is his father, who you say behaved so badly to him, still alive?"

"I believe so," Odetta answered, "but they say in Bourne that Mr. Worth has never forgiven him for what he made his family suffer, so it would, I think, be a mistake to mention him."

"Yes, of course," Lady Walmer agreed. "I was not thinking of doing so."

It was only a short drive to the Rue de la Paix, and as the horses came to a standstill outside No. 7, they saw that there were a large number of other smart carriages drawn up in the street.

Odetta began to understand Lady Walmer's feelings of apprehension in case Charles Worth had no time or in-

clination to add her to his list of distinguished, aristocrat-
ic, and Royal customers.

Odetta had also heard somebody tell her mother that
Worth also dressed actresses and the Courtesans who
had given the Second Empire a bad reputation over the
whole of Europe.

She was not supposed to be listening when this was
said, but she had read that there had always been great
Courtesans in France at the Royal Courts.

Thinking about it, she supposed that they, perhaps
more than anybody else, would wish to wear the beautiful creations that Worth designed individually for each
one of his customers.

They were shown upstairs by a very smart liveried
servant and ushered into a large Waiting-Room where
there were already a number of exceedingly smart women.

They looked the newcomers up and down with what
Odetta thought was a contemptuous and almost insolent
expression in their eyes.

Someone asked Lady Walmer's name, and she said in
quite good French:

"Please tell *Monsieur* Worth that Lady Walmer is here
to see him as a customer, and also to bring him messages
of affection from his friends and admirers in Bourne."

The servant repeated what she had said to make sure
he had it correct, and, gracefully spreading out the skirts
of her silk crinoline, Lady Walmer settled herself in one
of the gilt chairs that were arranged round the room.

Looking at the other ladies, Odetta saw for the first time
the new style which Charles Worth had introduced to
Paris.

Not one woman in the room, with the exception of
Lady Walmer and Penelope, wore a crinoline.

The cage of horse-hair, which had dominated fashionable gowns for so long, was gone.

In its place, the fullness of the gown was swept to the

back and the waist was dropped to the top of the hips.

It was so unusual, so sensational, that Odetta found herself staring at a lady opposite her until she received a freezing glance of disdain and quickly looked away.

They had waited for perhaps twenty minutes when the door at the end of the room opened and in a stentorian voice a servant called out:

"Lady Walmer!"

Odetta started because she was surprised, but Lady Walmer sprang to her feet eagerly.

Because she had not told them to stay where they were, Penelope and Odetta followed her into the next room.

Odetta was not quite certain what she expected, but certainly Mr. Worth did not look in the least as she had imagined he would.

He was reclining on a divan, a cigar between his lips, and he was wearing a flowing coat edged with fur at the neck, a floppy silk scarf instead of a cravat, and a velvet beret which, she was to learn later, he never removed.

He looked like an artist, and he had in fact modelled himself on Rembrandt.

Over-effusively because she was nervous, Lady Walmer was flattering him and telling him, her words almost falling over each other, how much he was admired, loved, and she might almost say "adored" by the people of Bourne.

"Where do you live, My Lady?" Charles Worth managed to ask when he could get a word in edgeways.

"My husband's home in The Hall at Edenham. We own a very large Estate. You may remember it from when you were a boy."

"Yes, I do," Charles Worth replied after a moment. "I presume, however, that it is not to discuss old times that you have come here to see me today, but for another reason."

"Of course!" Lady Walmer replied, and now her voice was almost ecstatic. "I want gowns, *Monsieur!* Dozens and dozens of new gowns in which I shall not be ashamed to meet the ladies of Paris, and also to have the privilege of showing your new fashions in England when I return home."

"Well, we must see what we can do for you. Where are you staying?"

"At the British Embassy. My husband is here on an important mission on behalf of the Prime Minister."

Listening, Odetta wondered if *Monsieur* Worth, who had every Queen in Europe beseeching him for gowns, was impressed.

But his eyes were inspecting Lady Walmer in the same way, she thought, that a man would take in the good points of a horse.

She had a very English beauty, and it struck Odetta, who was in one of her imaginative moods, that perhaps he thought his gowns could make her look like an English rose rather than the exotic birds-of-Paradise which the French beauties would resemble.

He snapped his fingers and an assistant appeared with lengths of extravagantly designed satins and brocades in pink, yellow, and green. There was also a silver tulle which made Odetta think of the stars in the Milky Way.

He spread it over his hands and said:

"I used this to dress Princess von Metternich and one spangled with gold for the Empress Elizabeth of Austria."

"It is lovely, absolutely lovely!" Lady Walmer enthused.

"It would suit you," Worth said, "but there are many sorts of tulle and we have to decide which will be the most effective."

The tulle was brought, and Odetta saw that there was shirred tulle as well as pleated tulle, draped tulle, puffed tulle, and layers of silk tulle, all of which, she felt, would give anybody who wore them an ethereal beauty as if they had stepped out of a dream.

Only after Lady Walmer had ordered two dozen gowns, without even asking the cost, did Worth turn his head towards Odetta and Penelope.

He had already promised Lady Walmer that if she would come back that afternoon, he would create a gown on her that she could wear that evening.

"I cannot even be seen until you dress me, *Monsieur,*" she had cried dramatically.

There was a smile on Charles Worth's lips that told her he agreed with her.

Now he asked:

"And these two young ladies?"

"My Stepdaughter requires two gowns," Lady Walmer said coldly. "Come and say: 'How do you do,' Penelope, to the greatest artist you are ever likely to meet."

Penelope rose obediently to curtsey to Mr. Worth, and he inclined his head condescendingly, then looked at Odetta.

"And the other young lady?"

"She is just a companion to my Stepdaughter," Lady Walmer said indifferently. "She is in Paris to help maid her, but otherwise she is of no consequence."

Charles Worth did not answer.

He looked at Odetta for a long moment as if, she thought, he would have liked to design a gown for her.

Then she told herself that she was once again being imaginative.

She had heard over and over again that Worth was interested in providing the best clothes only for the best people, and his prices were regulated accordingly.

It was only when they were driving back to the Embassy, with Lady Walmer talking excitedly of the gowns she intended to have, that Odetta felt just a little pang of envy.

If she could have just one fashionable gown, she thought
to herself, it would be better than feeling dowdy and
rather like somebody who had stepped out of Noah's
Ark.

Then she thought she was being very ungrateful to the
kind fate that had brought her to Paris when she had
least expected it. After all, what did it matter what she
looked like?

When they reached the Embassy they went upstairs,
and Emelene was waiting outside Her Ladyship's bedroom.

"Oh, Emelene, Emelene!" Lady Walmer exclaimed.
"You have never seen anything so fascinating, so wonderful as the clothes I am to have from *Monsieur* Worth. We
will need at least a dozen more trunks to convey them
back to London."

Emelene did not look over-pleased, but she had no
chance to speak as Lady Walmer went on:

"I shall be able to throw away everything I possess,
but everything, and start again! It is almost like being
reborn!"

The way she was talking made Odetta want to laugh,
but she felt it would be rude to do so, and she hurried
after Penelope, who had gone down the passage to her
own room.

"All this fuss about clothes!" she said scornfully as Odetta
joined her. "It would not matter what I wore if I were
walking in the woods with Simon or helping him with his
dogs."

"He will want you to look pretty," Odetta said firmly.
"Every man wants to be proud of the woman he loves."

Penelope looked startled.

"I had not thought of that."

"I think you are very lucky," Odetta went on, "and I
am sure when you get home and show Simon your new
gowns he will admire you even more than he does now. I
have never liked you in a crinoline."

Penelope jumped up and went to the long mirror which was attached to the wardrobe door.

She stood staring at her reflection. Then she said:

"I look a mess! I always do!"

"You will look very pretty in the new line," Odetta said reassuringly. "For one thing, it will make you look thinner and taller."

Penelope's eyes lit up.

"If I am going to look pretty for Simon, I am quite prepared to endure those fittings."

"You are being sensible," Odetta said. "But try to persuade your father to give you not two gowns but several more. They may have to last you a long time."

Penelope looked at her in a startled fashion, then she realised that Odetta was suggesting that if she did run away with Simon and they had very little money, she would certainly not be able to afford another Worth gown.

"You are right!" Penelope cried. "Of course you are! I will coax Papa into giving me quite a lot of gowns. I am afraid I was not very grateful when he said he would give me two."

Odetta looked at the clock.

"Luncheon will be ready in a very short time," she said, "and your father might be waiting downstairs alone. Why not go and talk to him now?"

Penelope walked across the room to kiss her.

"You are so sensible, Odetta," she said. "I love being with you."

Then, throwing down on the bed the bonnet she had worn, she went from the room and Odetta heard her rather heavy footsteps running down the passage towards the staircase.

She gave a little sigh and went to her own bedroom to tidy herself, and wondered whether Hannah and she together could try to copy the lovely gowns she had seen at Worth's, and their exquisite materials.

There had been sketches propped up all round his rooms, and they had been so lovely that she was quite certain that even if they could afford the materials, she and Hannah would never be able to produce anything that resembled them in the slightest.

"Never mind about clothes," she told herself sensibly. "I am in Paris, and I must make opportunities to see as much of the city as I can."

At the same time, as she caught a glimpse of herself in the mirror, she knew that it was a good thing she was not lunching downstairs with the Ambassador and his guests, for there was no doubt that she looked like Cinderella, and a very dowdy one at that.

* * *

"All I can say," Emelene said sharply, "is that this new fashion's costing me a great deal of money!"

As she spoke, she roughly pulled several of Lady Walmer's gowns out of the wardrobe and threw them on the floor, as she replaced them with the gowns that had arrived from the Rue de la Paix.

Odetta, who was sitting talking to her as she sewed some lace on one of Penelope's petticoats, understood why she was so disagreeable.

She had known for years that one of the perks of a lady's-maid was to be able to sell the gowns which her mistress had discarded.

She had read in a magazine that twice a year the Empress gave her discarded gowns to her lady's-maid, who sold them to people in America and also to places in Paris whose business was to lend or hire them.

When she had first learnt of this, Odetta had questioned her father, and he had told her that for centuries, officials and servants at Court had the right to acquire the clothes of the Monarch and his Consort when their wardrobes were renewed.

"There are various references in my books," he had said. "I can show you examples where there was a great deal of trouble when they were denied what they considered one of their perks."

It was after that that Odetta learnt that in stately homes on both sides of the Channel and even in bourgeois residences, in fact wherever servants were employed, they expected to acquire the cast-off garments of their employers.

Because her father found that it interested her, he looked it up in his Library and found a *Punch* published over twenty years earlier in which the Correspondent from France had written:

> *The Empress sets an example by giving every robe once worn to her attendants. As these are of course sold again, all Paris overflows with the Imperial defroque. A few nights ago on the boards of one of the theatres there was recognized a brocade that had lately figured on the throne.*

Odetta had laughed at the time and thought it very funny, but now she felt sorry for Emelene, for she was well aware that the new fashions would, as she had said herself, cost her a lot of money since gowns made in the old style would be worthless.

"I tell you what I will do," Odetta said impulsively. "I will try to alter some of the gowns for you. I am sure if we swept the skirts to the back and dropped down the waist a little, you would be able to sell them, if not at the top price then at least for quite a decent sum, since the material is so beautiful."

Emelene looked surprised.

"Could you really do that, *M'mselle?*" she asked. "I never was much use as a dressmaker, but you certainly sew beautifully."

"Thank you," Odetta said with a smile, "and I will

alter the gowns if I can. Which one would you like me to start on?"

"Try this one," Emelene replied.

It was a lovely gown of very pale blue satin overlaid with tulle in the same colour, with long ribbons hanging from the waist, which had billowed out over the wide crinoline.

It was a gown which was really too young for Lady Walmer, but she had looked very beautiful in it, although blue did not become her as well as other colours.

Odetta picked up the garment and examined it critically.

"There are masses of stuff in this to make what will look like a bustle at the back. I am sure I can do something with it."

"I should be very grateful if you could," Emelene said. "Fit it on yourself, *M'mselle*. It's a pity you can't wear some of these lovely gowns, but then where do you go to be seen in them?"

"Where indeed?" Odetta replied. "But I am not complaining. I am so happy to be here, and I hope I shall be able to see a lot more of Paris before we leave."

"It's easy to do that, *M'mselle*, Emelene said. "I suggest you take Miss Penelope out driving. The stables are full of horses and carriages. You only have to ask for one."

"We will do that, and thank you, Emelene."

"I should thank you, *M'mselle*, for offering to alter the gowns for me."

"I will take this one to my room," Odetta said, "and, as my wardrobe is practically empty, why do you not put those you want me to alter in there? I will have a chance to look at them whenever I am free and see what can be done."

"It's a pleasure, *M'mselle*," Emelene said. "Not many young ladies would be as kind to me as you are."

Odetta merely smiled, and, folding the gown over her arm, carried it to her bedroom.

Even if they were now old-fashioned, she thought, it was lovely to be able to look at clothes that were so beautiful, and they added a new lustre to the fanciful tales she told herself about the Balls and Receptions that were taking place in Paris whilst she sat in the Embassy and sewed.

During the next two or three days there was little chance to see anything but the inside of No. 7 Rue de la Paix.

Penelope had persuaded her father to give her not two gowns but ten, and because Lady Walmer had said firmly that neither she nor her Stepdaughter would go anywhere until they were properly dressed, there were fittings from first thing in the morning until dinner-time, with only a break for luncheon.

Even Odetta grew tired of looking at materials, for what she wanted to see was the Seine, the Bois, the new fountains in the Place de la Concorde, and the Cathedral of Notre Dame.

But one by one the gowns were ready, and Lady Walmer was out for luncheon and dinner, while Penelope was included in the dinner-parties and the Balls afterwards.

"I want to go home," was all she could say. "If I have to dance I want to dance with Simon."

"I know," Odetta said sympathetically, "but try to be nice to the people you meet. You never know when one of them may be useful to you. Perhaps they may be able to find something for Simon to do if you run away with no money."

Penelope looked at her in astonishment. Then she said:

"Of course! That is a good idea! Why should we not come to France, where it would be difficult for Papa to find us?"

"One never knows what might turn up," Odetta said, "so you must make yourself charming to your partners tonight, Penelope, and to the older people when you are introduced to them. There is no telling what might come from such encounters."

Odetta was thinking that, like in a fairy-story, Penelope would find a rich patron of some sort for Simon, who would be given a new importance, and Lord Walmer would then welcome him as a son-in-law.

Even though she admitted to herself that this was just a little more of her make-believe, she knew that she had inspired Penelope into being far more pleasant and agreeable than she would otherwise have been to the people she met.

'If I could only go to just one party,' she thought to herself, as Penelope ran downstairs in a new gown of deep strawberry pink, which with her dark hair and clear skin made her look not only pretty but very much more elegant than she had ever looked before.

Then with a little sigh Odetta went back to her bedroom, where her supper was waiting for her on a tray.

On the bed she saw lying three more gowns that Emelene had brought for her to alter.

Chapter Three

Odetta stared at her reflection in the mirror and gave a little cry of delight.

"I have done it! I have really done it!"

She turned first this way, then the other, looking at herself in the blue gown that Emelene had given her first.

She had altered it so that it really looked as if it had come straight from Worth.

She had dropped the waistline, and the stiff folds of the crinoline had all been swept back to end in a short train.

Odetta had then arranged the tulle over it to give it an ethereal appearance, and the blue ribbons which had decorated the crinoline were also at the back.

It had been difficult to slip the bodice off the shoulders but she had achieved it, and she thought that her own waist had never looked smaller.

She also had no idea that she had such a good figure until the tightness of the bodice revealed it.

'Emeline will be delighted!' she thought, and swirled round in front of the mirror as if she were dancing.

Even as she did so, she heard music.

She knew it came from the house next door to the

Embassy, where Lord and Lady Walmer and Penelope were tonight attending a Masked Ball.

"I wish you were coming with me," Penelope had said when she was dressed in one of her new gowns.

Odetta had tied a small lace-edged black mask over her eyes.

"I wish I were too," she said honestly, "but I will make up a story that you dance with a handsome Prince and are the Belle of the Ball."

"I want to dance with Simon," Penelope said. "I wish he were here tonight. I am sure he would admire me in my new gown."

"Of course he would!" Odetta agreed. "But there will be plenty of other people to do so, so enjoy yourself and learn new and exciting things to say to Simon."

Penelope refused to be enthused.

"I just want to tell him that I love him," she said miserably.

When she was ready, Odetta went to the top of the stairs to watch her join Lord and Lady Walmer in the Hall.

Lady Walmer was wearing fancy-dress but had said quite firmly that there was no time to buy one for Penelope.

Worth had created for her a costume of a shepherdess modelled on a figure in Sèvres porcelain, and Odetta could not help thinking that nobody could look prettier.

The dress was of pale pink, garlanded with pom-poms of roses caught up with silver tassels.

She noticed that Lady Walmer's mask was little more than a piece of ribbon edged with lace, and the holes in it were large enough to show off her blue eyes.

Lord Walmer was in ordinary evening-clothes but as Penelope joined them he enquired:

"Not in fancy-dress?"

"She looks very nice as she is," Lady Walmer said

quickly, "and a great many people will not be dressed up."

"Me for one!" Lord Walmer replied. "Like the Emperor, I consider it beneath my dignity!"

"I certainly agree with you," said the Ambassador, who had walked into the Hall at that moment, "but it will add to the gaiety of the proceedings if we wear Venetian cloaks with our evening-dress, and I have one for you, My Lord."

"That is very kind of you," Lord Walmer replied.

"One advantage of this Ball," the Ambassador continued, "is that we can come home quickly as soon as we are bored."

"How can we do that?" Lord Walmer enquired.

"Because the *Comte*'s garden adjoins ours," the Ambassador explained. "There is a gate between the two gardens which is usually kept locked. But tonight it will be open, and I can assure you that I shall not stay late."

Lord Walmer smiled.

"Nor shall I."

"I think you are a pair of spoil-sports!" Lady Walmer complained. "I have every intention of dancing until dawn."

"I am sure, My Lady, you will not lack for partners to enable you to do so," Lord Lyons said rather heavily. "But as we do not wish to be late for dinner, I suggest we drive the short distance to the *Comte*'s front door. We have to arrive in style."

They laughed at this, and then Lady Walmer led the way to the carriages.

Odetta gave a little sigh and went back to her bedroom.

While she was watching everybody leave, her dinner had been brought upstairs and was waiting for her on a table by the window.

She knew she was lucky in that the Chef always provided her with two delicious dishes and a small bottle of wine to accompany them.

She had seen the food prepared by the staff at the Hall for Penelope's Governesses and was aware that they took little trouble over anyone who did not eat in the Dining-Room.

When she had eaten her meal and was finishing off the blue gown, Odetta was imagining what the Masked Ball would look like next door and wondering what costumes the more important guests would wear.

She had heard that at one Ball, the Princess von Metternich, who was responsible for bringing *redoutes* into fashion in the 1860s, had appeared as a milk-maid with silver buckets.

At the first Ball she gave, which was in honour of the Empress, everybody had to be masked, including the Emperor, who had worn a Venetian cloak while his wife went disguised as Juno.

Mr. Sheffield, who had told Odetta about it, had said that it took place in the Austrian Embassy and a special Ball-Room had been erected in the garden for the occasion, its walls decorated with large mirrors and covered in light blue satin.

"Oh, I wish the Ambassador would give a Ball like that here!" Odetta had exclaimed.

"I am afraid that is unlikely," Mr. Sheffield replied. "His Excellency dislikes dancing and is known never to take any exercise except to walk as far as the Church on the other side of the road."

Odetta had laughed, but all the same she wished that the Ambassador were more socially minded.

Although Lord and Lady Walmer went to parties every night, very few people seemed to be entertained in the Embassy.

Although she knew she would not have been able to take part in them, Odetta thought that at least she could

have watched them through the bannisters at the top of
the staircase.

Now, as she heard the music of Offenbach wafting through
her window from the garden next door, she imagined she
was dancing with some tall and handsome stranger.

Of course, she would not be Odetta Charlwood—Miss
Nobody from Nowhere. She would be a French *Princesse*.

She thought for a moment, then decided her name
would be "Charleval," which was near enough to "Charlwood."

As she moved gracefully in time to the waltz, she told
herself that her husband, the Prince, who was much
older than she was, was unfortunately unable to accompany her to the Ball because he was ill.

"But you must go and enjoy yourself, my dearest," he
would say. "I want all Paris to see how lovely you are,
and I think that gown becomes you better than anything
else you have ever worn."

"That is sweet of you, Jean," she replied.

He kissed her hand.

"You know above everything else that I love you," he
said. "Now go!"

She bent and kissed his cheek, then she left the room
to walk down the stairs with her silk train rustling behind
her to where the carriage bearing her husband's coat-of-
arms was waiting to carry her to the Masked Ball.

Odetta's eyes were half-closed and her lips were smiling,
and only when she bumped into the end of the bed did
she feel as if she awoke with a start.

She was not *la Princesse de Charleval*. She was just
Odetta Charlwood, who had come to Paris to maid her
friend, Penelope, and like Cinderella she had been left
behind while everyone else went to the Ball.

She gave a little sigh and thought:

'I wish I had a Fairy-Godmother.'

It was at that moment that an idea came to her that

was so outrageous and so revolutionary that she laughed at herself for even thinking of it.

Then as the music seemed to grow louder, she looked at herself in the mirror and impulsively went next door into Penelope's bedroom.

On the dressing-table, where they had been left because Odetta had not yet put them away, were several masks.

Mr. Sheffield had produced a whole box of them so that Lady Walmer could have first choice of the one she liked best, then Emelene had brought them to Penelope's room.

"Here you are, *M'mselle*," she had said, giving them to Odetta. "There will be a large number of people at the party tonight who will look much better incognito than when they are not!"

It was a sharp sort of comment that Emelene often made, and with a little laugh, because it was expected of her, Odetta took the box, hoping Penelope had not heard.

But she had.

"It does not matter what anyone thinks I look like except Simon," she remarked.

"Of course not," Odetta agreed, "and Emelene was not talking about you. I am sure there are lots of really ugly people in France who find it fun to be incognito, and the ladies who are out to enjoy themselves are able to flirt without being criticised by the Dowagers."

She had deliberately chosen a very pretty mask for Penelope, but the one she had liked best had been too small for her.

Now she picked it up and put it over her own eyes and thought it made her look mysterious and very different from the way she appeared ordinarily.

Since she had been in Paris she had been arranging her hair in a much more fashionable way, with ringlets at the back of her head.

She felt that Lady Walmer looked at her critically, but

as she never went anywhere or met anybody, there was no reason for Her Ladyship to complain.

Now with her bare shoulders encircled with the softness of tulle, her fair curls seemed to pick up the light, and she would have been very stupid if she had not realised that the picture she made was a very alluring one.

"But I cannot do anything so outrageous!" she said aloud. "It would be wrong."

"Wrong for whom?" "Who would be hurt?" "Who would know?"

The questions presented themselves one after another, and suddenly she smiled and there were dimples on each side of her mouth.

"It is an opportunity that may never come again," she said aloud. "I will do it!"

She took one more look at her reflection, then she went back to her own bedroom.

In the small jewel-case that she always kept with her, because it was so precious, was her mother's wedding-ring.

She slipped it onto her finger and knew there was something else she must do as well.

She tip-toed along the passage and went into Lady Walmer's room and saw, as she had expected, that it was very neat and tidy.

Emelene had already told her that as soon as Her Ladyship had left, she was going out to see her friends and relations.

"There'll be no need for me to get back before dawn," she had said. "You can be sure Her Ladyship'll not leave the Ball until there's no-one left to dance with her."

"Is there anything I can do for you?" Odetta had asked.

"*Non, merci,*" Emelene had replied. "But it's like your kindness, *M'mselle*, to ask me. It is something I'll not forget."

Odetta went now across the room to the dressing-table.

She knew what she was looking for and found it immediately: an elegant box in which there was a pink salve which Lady Walmer applied to her lips.

Odetta had noticed that the ladies in Mr. Worth's Waiting-Room, from the *Grandes Dames* to the actresses and the Courtesans, accentuated their beauty with cosmetics, and Lady Walmer was no exception.

Skilfully, Odetta reddened her own lips and applied a slight dusting of powder to her fair skin.

She did not really need it, but knew she would look strange without it.

With her heart beating rapidly at her own daring, she went from the bedroom, shutting the door behind her.

The only real danger was that she might be seen by one of the staff, but she was quite sure, since the Ambassador was out, that the servants would be below-stairs.

Not even the footmen would be on duty in the Hall until there was a likelihood of their Master returning.

She was right.

There was nobody to see her come down the curved staircase, holding on to the wrought-iron bannisters, to slip out to the garden through the door at the back of the house.

The green lawns were like velvet under her satin slippers, and she moved in the shadows of the trees until beyond the wide flower-beds she found a gate which led into the next-door garden.

The music that had grown louder and louder guided her, and also through the leaves of the trees she could see the lights that she found later were Chinese lanterns.

As she stepped into the next garden, she took a path which led her through some thick shrubs. Soon she could see that a dance-floor had been erected at the far end of the garden.

It was below some stone steps leading from the house,

and dancing was in progress also in the huge lighted Ball-Room on the first floor.

Now she drew in her breath with excitement, for, just as she had imagined so often, the women in their lovely gowns had not only the grace of swans but also, because so many were in fancy-dress, they looked like an aviary of exotic birds.

She had meant to stand in the shadows and watch, but, because it was so fascinating, she moved a little nearer so that she could see more clearly.

There were costumes of every sort and description, from a Venetian with black skirts caught up by diamonds to reveal an under-skirt of scarlet satin, to a Louis XV equestrian costume.

A number of ladies obviously fancied themselves as Marie Antoinette, and there were dozens of Pierrots.

One costume which Odetta knew unmistakably had been designed by Worth was of white tulle spangled with silver, and its wearer had a huge diamond star on her head. As she waltzed she seemed a vision of celestial beauty.

The garden dance-floor was growing fuller as more people came down the steps from the indoor Ball-Room to seek the cool of the garden.

Odetta was staring entranced at a lady wearing the head-dress of a small peacock and a train decorated with peacock plumes, when a voice said beside her:

"Are you waiting for some laggard partner, or have you just dropped down from the sky to bemuse us poor mortals?"

The words were spoken in English, but in a mocking voice that sounded cynical and at the same time blasé.

She looked round hastily and saw standing at her side a tall Gentleman who seemed for the moment not to be real.

He was wearing a mask and had a Venetian cloak over his shoulders, and she thought, not only because he had spoken in English but also from something in his appearance, that he obviously was of British nationality.

Odetta's first impulse was to run away. Then, almost as if her own day-dreams submerged her ordinary self, she found herself thinking of how a *Princesse* would reply, and after a short pause she answered in French:

"*Je suis seule, Monsieur.*"

"Nevertheless, I am quite certain you speak very good English," the Gentleman replied, "and so we will talk in my language. I find it easier!"

Odetta could not help smiling.

She thought that most Englishmen found it difficult to achieve a correct French pronunciation.

"Will you dance with me?" the Gentleman asked.

Just for a second Odetta thought she should refuse.

Then as if once again the *Princesse* took over from the nervous "Miss Nobody from Nowhere," she replied:

"*Merci, Monsieur.* I would like to dance in this beautiful garden."

As she spoke she walked towards the dance-floor, conscious of her train moving gracefully behind her and knowing that her mask would make it impossible for Lady Walmer or even Penelope to recognise her.

Her partner put his arm round her waist and took her hand in his.

As they took the first steps, Odetta realised that the Orchestra was playing a Strauss waltz, and it seemed to make everything even more romantic than it was already.

The stars overhead, the Chinese lanterns hanging from the boughs of the trees, the glitter of chandeliers in the Ball-Room, and the profusion of exotic and beautiful gowns made her certain that she had stepped into one of her own dreams.

They danced in silence and she found that her partner

danced well, but it was not difficult for her to follow him.

Penelope had had dancing-lessons from a teacher who came to the Hall twice a week, and Odetta had learnt at the same time.

She had been aware that the teacher found her an exceptionally bright pupil, while poor Penelope was heavy, clumsy, and kept forgetting her steps.

Now to dance with a Gentleman who was young and tall was an enchantment in itself.

"You are so light," he said halfway round the floor, "that I feel I was right and you have flown down from the sky to join the revelry."

"And of course I must fly back on the stroke of midnight!" Odetta laughed.

"I hope you will do nothing of the sort," her partner replied.

He spoke in the same dry, cynical manner as he had before, and she was not certain whether it was a compliment or not.

When the dance came to an end they moved off the floor and walked almost instinctively into the shade of one of the great trees.

There was a seat beneath it and as they sat down a liveried servant offered them glasses of champagne.

This was something Odetta had drunk only once or twice in her life, but she took a glass, feeling that to drink champagne was also part of this enchanted evening.

Her partner drank a little from his glass, then he turned sideways in his seat to say to her:

"Now, tell me about yourself."

"You mean that I should describe my place in the firmament?" Odetta asked with a very convincing French accent. "Shall I tell you that I came from the Milky Way, or perhaps from a planet?"

"It will have to be from Venus."

Odetta laughed.

"Perhaps, *Monsieur,* it would be better if you told me why you are in Paris."

"The answer to that is surely obvious. To meet beautiful women like you!"

"That evades the question very skilfully."

"You think I wish to evade it just as you are evading telling me about yourself? Let us start from the beginning. What is your name?"

Without thinking, Odetta replied:

"Odetta."

"It is a lovely name, but what else?"

"Tonight we are supposed to be incognito. That is why we wear masks."

"So you really are determined to be evasive. Then let me assure you, I shall make it my business to know your secrets."

"Why should you be interested?"

"Do you really want an answer to that?"

"*Naturellement!*"

The way she spoke made the Gentleman smile.

"You sound as if you are greedy for compliments," he said. "Looking at you, I am sure that you are satiated with them already, and I am not as eloquent as a Frenchman would be."

"I suppose my answer to that should be to reassure you in case you develop a feeling of inferiority."

As she spoke she thought it would be very good for the rather cynical Gentleman to be teased, because she had the feeling, although she had no idea why, that he was too awe-inspiring for such a thing to have happened to him in the past.

"It is certainly something of which I have not been accused before," he replied. "In fact, I believe my reputation is that I am overbearing and autocratic."

"And are you?"

"I hope so. I have no use for people who are humble

and subservient because they do not believe in themselves."

Odetta was amused.

She supposed he had no idea that it was difficult to be anything but humble if one was poor and of no consequence, and as to feeling subservient, she was quite sure that the Gentleman talking to her would find any other attitude impertinent.

Her dimples must have shown in her cheeks, for after a moment he said:

"I have the feeling that you are laughing at me, which I am not certain if I like or dislike."

"Perhaps when you wear a mask you are not so intimidating as when you can annihilate with an icy glance anybody who offends you."

Now the Gentleman laughed.

"Are you afraid that might happen to you?"

"Of course," Odetta said, "I am terrified! I can see you are a very overwhelming person, but then Englishmen often are."

"How many Englishmen do you know?"

Odetta thought she had been rather indiscreet.

She had been carefully talking in an assumed French accent, and now she made a typically French gesture with her hands as she replied:

"How can I count them?"

The Gentleman caught her left hand in his.

She had taken off her gloves after they had sat down on the seat, to make it easier for her to hold her glass of champagne, and now looking at her wedding-ring he asked:

"So you are married? Is your husband here?"

"No, he is at home," Odetta replied. "*Pauvre Jean, il est malade.*"

"So you came here on your own, I suppose to see what fun you could find in his absence."

Odetta took her hand from his.

"I think you are assuming, *Monsieur*, a great many things that have no foundation in fact and anyway should not concern you."

The Gentleman did not speak, and she said:

"Perhaps I should go back to my friends."

She made a little gesture as if she would rise, but the Gentleman's hand came out to hold on to her wrist and prevent her from doing so.

"Do not leave me," he said. "I will apologise if I have offended you, but I want you to stay with me."

"Why? There must be many ladies here with whom you could be dancing."

"There is only one little star that has fallen down from the sky in whom I am interested."

Odetta drew in her breath.

The fact that he was holding her hand had given her a strange feeling, and now she told herself it was very intriguing and very exciting to have a man speak to her with what for the moment was a note of sincerity in his voice.

This was exactly the sort of conversation she had imagined in her dreams.

She had replied so far in the way that she thought the *Princesse* would, assuming a sophistication and wittiness that she was sure would be the inevitable part of such an encounter.

"Have you forgiven me?" the Gentleman asked.

"Because it is such a lovely night, it would be difficult to do anything else."

"I am not particularly concerned with the night, but if it will mediate on my behalf, then I accept its help most gratefully."

There was a little pause, then he asked:

"Will you dance with me again?"

"I suppose, conventionally, I should say 'no.' "

"I want you to say 'yes,' and I have no intention of

allowing you to dance with anybody else. So, Odetta, you will have to give in gracefully."

"Now you are definitely being overbearing."

"I must live up to my reputation," the Gentleman said loftily.

They went back to the dance-floor, and now it seemed to Odetta as if not only their feet moved in unison.

Even when they were silent they were talking to each other in a manner which made her feel that their words sparkled and glittered like the people moving round them and the stars overhead.

This time whem they left the floor the Gentleman said:

"I think we should have supper while it is still early. Later it may be difficult to find a table."

"That would be pleasant," Odetta agreed.

They walked to another part of the garden where there were some tables laid out under the trees, each lit by one red candle, which gave those who were supping the impression that they were isolated on a small, intimate island.

The Gentleman led the way to a table away from the others, and Odetta was glad that, whatever his reason, she would not appear too conspicuous.

Waiters brought them caviar and poured out glasses of champagne.

Then as Odetta looked round her, intrigued by the attraction of the Supper-Room and the costumes of the other guests, she was aware that her partner was not eating or drinking but just sitting looking at her.

She glanced at him enquiringly and wondered what he would look like without his mask.

He had a square chin, a determined, rather hard mouth, and by the light from the candle she could see there were undoubtedly lines of cynicism running from the sides of his nostrils down to the edge of his lips.

Suddenly he smiled, and it seemed to transform his face.

"Is it possible that you are curious?" he asked.

"As to who you are, *Monsieur?*" Odetta replied quickly. "It can be of little consequence, as you live on the other side of the Channel."

"But at the moment I am here," he said, "close to you, and when we were dancing I felt that we were very close indeed."

"Now I have the idea," Odetta said, "that you are deliberately behaving like a Frenchman, *Monsieur.* I am sure an Englishman would never say such things to someone he had met for the first time."

"You are quite right in thinking that," the Gentleman replied, "but tonight it is difficult to remember that as an Englishman I should be cold, reserved, and inarticulate."

Odetta laughed.

"I am sure that is something you could never be!"

"That is where you are wrong," he replied. "And may I tell you that when I came here tonight, I told myself it would be an extraordinarily boring evening and I would leave at the first opportunity."

"Why? Why should you feel like that?"

"Because I had no wish to come to Paris in the first place, and if there is one thing I find a bore, it is men and women making fools of themselves by dressing up like a lot of Circus performers!"

There was no doubt that his tone was scathing, and because it seemed somehow to jar on the beauty of the garden and the excitement she was feeling, Odetta said quickly:

"Do not . . . speak like . . . that."

"Why not?"

"Because you are spoiling the evening for me. I am finding the party very exciting and very lovely. I want to enjoy every moment of it; and it will be something to . . . remember."

There was silence for a moment, then the Gentleman said:

"You speak as though this is all very new to you—or are you going away?"

He was perceptive, Odetta thought, and it was dangerous.

"I . . . I just want to . . . enjoy myself," she said quickly.

"I will not spoil it for you, but you have made me even more curious than I was before."

The waiters brought more food, but Odetta ate without thinking and without even tasting what she was eating.

She wanted to impress everything round her on her mind and memory, and it was also exciting to know that she had intrigued the man next to her and that his eyes never left her face.

"Would you like to dance again?" he asked.

She realised with a little start that they must have been sitting for a long time at the supper-table and the people round them had come and gone and others had taken their places.

"What is the time?" Odetta asked.

The Gentleman looked at the gold watch in his waist-coat pocket.

"Nearly half-past-one."

Odetta gave a little cry.

"So late? I told you that like Cinderella I had to leave at midnight."

"Well, if your coach has by now turned back into a pumpkin, you are certainly not in rags, and the glass slippers are still on your feet."

Odetta smiled.

"You know your fairy-stories!"

"I was brought up on them, as I imagine you were."

"But of course! And *Cinderella*, which I must point out was written by a Frenchman, has always been my favourite."

"I cannot imagine you sitting at home like Cinderella while your ugly sisters went to the Ball."

Odetta found herself smiling. He had no idea how near to the truth that was.

She did not speak and after a moment he said:

"What are you keeping from me, apart from your name? Do you not feel that we know each other well enough now for you to tell me the truth?"

"If I do, you might be disappointed. We have met at a Masked Ball, and it might be very disillusioning if we took off our masks and our anonymity."

"I doubt that," the Gentleman replied. "Give me your hand."

As he spoke, he held out his hand, and without even thinking Odetta laid her fingers on it.

He covered them with his other hand and there was something in the warmth of his palms and the closeness of his clasp that gave her a strange feeling.

Then he said in a low voice:

"You must know without my telling you that I want to see you again. So let us stop playing games, and I will start by telling you that I am the Earl of Houghton!"

Odetta gave a little start. Then she stared at him incredulously through her mask.

The Earl would not have expected her to have heard of him, but she had done so, and in a very different manner from what he might have thought.

It seemed an extraordinary, incredible quirk of fate that the stranger she should have met so casually at a Ball to which she had not been invited, and which she had no right to attend, should be a man she disliked the thought of, even though she had never met him.

Her mother had been a very distant relative of the Earl.

"A cousin at least a dozen times removed," she had said once. "Nevertheless, I am proud of my Houghton blood, or I was."

Odetta had known that she spoke in the past tense for the simple reason that seven or perhaps eight years ago her mother had decided that her father should move from the Parish of Edenham to a living that could provide him with a better salary.

"We have lived here ever since we first married," she had said to Odetta, "and although I have been happy, very happy with your father, I cannot help feeling that he is wasting his brains and his personality in such a tiny village where he has nobody of his own intellect and ability with whom to talk."

"What are you going to do about it?" Odetta had asked.

She felt as she spoke that her mother was following her own train of thought. Then she said:

"As there is no better living free in this Diocese at the moment—and if there were one I doubt if your father would get it—I have a very good mind to write to the Earl of Houghton."

"As he is a relation, I am sure he would help you, Mama," Odetta said reassuringly.

"I have not met the present Earl since he was a small child," her mother replied. "Nevertheless, I was a Houghton before I married, and blood is supposed to be thicker than water."

"Does the Earl have many livings at his disposal?" Odetta asked.

Her mother nodded.

"He is very rich, very powerful, and I am sure he has dozens!" she said. "Perhaps he will think it impertinent of me to approach him, but 'nothing ventured, nothing gained.' "

She laughed as she spoke, then sat down to open her writing-box.

"What will Papa say about this?" Odetta asked.

Her mother laughed.

"Your father is the most unworldly, least ambitious man I have ever known. He wants nothing he has not got already, which is his wife, his daughter, and his books."

Her mother sighed.

"But I want a great deal more, not for myself, my dearest, but for you. In a few years you will be very pretty, and I want you to have all the things I had when I was young."

"Were your relatives very angry with you when you married Papa?"

"Of course they were," her mother replied. "They thought, as I was so pretty, that I ought to marry somebody very important and very rich. But I loved your father and he loved me and nothing else mattered."

Odetta had watched her mother writing the letter and, after it was sent, waiting impatiently for a reply.

When it came and her mother had read the letter, she had been angry.

It was something she seldom was, and Odetta, watching her face, asked apprehensively:

"What has upset you, Mama?"

"This letter," her mother replied.

"Is it from the Earl of Houghton?"

"It is, and you may read it, if you wish."

Her mother put it down on the table beside her, then walked out of the room, and Odetta knew it was to hide the tears which had come to her eyes.

The letter was very short, and she read:

Dear Mrs. Charlwood:

I have received the letter You wrote to me on behalf of your Husband, the Reverend Arthur

Charlwood, asking if I would consider Him when a
vacancy arises in the livings on my Estate.

My father always warned me that to favour Rel-
atives was a mistake, as They were invariably both
critical and ungrateful. I intend, now that I am
Head of the Family, to follow his example and his
advice.

Yours sincerely,
Houghton

Odetta had read it and felt as angry as her mother had
been.

Because she knew it was both a disappointment and a
snub, they had neither of them ever mentioned the Earl
again.

Now as he held her hand she told herself that she
hated him, and if she could hurt him in the way he had
hurt her mother and indirectly her father, although he
had no knowledge of it, she would be willing to do so.

Once again her dream-world seemed to envelop her
and she knew that the man beside her was the villain
who would finally be unmasked and punished for his
treachery.

She wondered how the *Princesse* de Charleval would
treat him, and knew what she must do.

Almost instinctively her fingers moved a little in his
clasp and she said:

"*Tiens!* But you are indeed very important, *Milord!* I
too have a position in France, but I am aware you will not
have heard of me."

"Tell me your name."

"My husband is *le Prince* Jean de Charleval."

"So you are a *Princesse!* It is what I might have expected,
and *Princesse* Odetta is a lovely name for a very lovely
person."

"Once again you are flattering me, *Monsieur*."

"No, I am speaking the truth. When can we meet again?"

Odetta shrugged her shoulders, conscious as she did so that the blue tulle moved softly against the whiteness of her skin.

She knew the Earl had noticed, and he said:

"You know as well as I do that we have to talk to each other. Will you have luncheon with me?"

Odetta shook her head.

"Then dinner or supper?"

Odetta forced herself to think of what was planned for Lord and Lady Walmer, and she remembered almost as if it were emblazoned in front of her in letters of fire that tomorrow night the Ambassador was taking them and Penelope to the Tuileries Palace.

They were to dine with the Emperor and Empress at a large dinner that was being given for the members of the Commission with which Lord Walmer was involved.

"You can manage dinner?" the Earl asked insistently.

"I . . . I think so . . . but I believe I should say 'no.' "

"But instead, because I want you to dine with me and I want to talk to you, and there are so many things I have to say, you will come?"

"Perhaps . . . if it is . . . possible."

"Then where can I call for you?"

"You must not do that. It would be . . . how do you say . . . very unconventional for us to . . . dine alone."

"Then how we can meet?"

Odetta thought swiftly.

Then she remembered that if there was a gate from the Embassy into this garden, there was also a gate, for she had seen it, leading out into the road outside.

She was silent for a moment before she said:

"If you will wait in a carriage for me in the Rue de

Pierre at half-past-eight o'clock, I will join you . . . if it is . . . possible."

"If it is possible?" the Earl repeated. "It *has* to be possible! If you do not come, I will search all Paris for you. Somebody will know where you live."

"I doubt if you will find me," Odetta replied. "We are staying with friends."

"I understand," the Earl answered, "and you do not wish your friends to know that you are with me."

"No, of course not! They would be very . . . shocked."

"Then you must make some plausible excuse. But I promise, Odetta, I intend to see you again, and nothing and nobody shall stop me!"

There was a note of sincerity in his voice that was very unlike the cynical way he had spoken to her at first, and Odetta smiled secretly to herself.

Her imagination was already weaving a plot in which she would discomfort the Earl and avenge his behaviour to her mother.

She rose to her feet.

"Let us dance," she said. "Perhaps later in the evening you will change your mind and not wish to see me again."

"You know that is a very foolish statement," the Earl answered. "I want it more than I can possibly express in words, or at any rate in English."

"Try French instead," Odetta said with a smile, as they walked between the tables towards the dance-floor.

"No," the Earl replied. "I will leave it instead to the beat of your heart and mine, and the feeling that when I hold you in my arms it will be impossible for you ever to escape them."

The way he spoke made Odetta suddenly feel frightened. She felt almost as if he was taking her mind away from her and she could no longer think for herself.

They waltzed round the floor, then she said:

"How stupid of me! I have left my handkerchief on the table."

"Is it important to you?"

"It is a very pretty one and I should hate to lose it."

"Then I suppose I must fetch it," he said. "I will not be more than a minute."

"I am sorry to be such a . . . trouble."

"You could not be that," he replied.

He walked round the edge of the floor until he was out of sight, then Odetta sprang to her feet.

Moving swiftly, she found her way under the trees into the shrubs which hid the gate into the Embassy garden.

It was open and she slipped through it, then hurried across the lawn.

Because she was so late, she was afraid that perhaps the garden-door had been locked and she would not be able to get into the house. Then she told herself she was being needlessly apprehensive.

Lady Walmer would not have thought of coming home so early and her only real danger was that she might encounter His Lordship or the Ambassador.

However, there was nobody about and she slipped up the stairs and found her way to her bedroom.

She wondered whether or not Penelope was back and thought it was unlikely. Anyway, it would be a mistake for anyone to know what she had been doing.

She stood looking at herself in the mirror, then as she took off her mask she saw that her eyes were shining, her cheeks were flushed, and her lips were still red with the salve she had applied to them.

"It has been an adventure! And the most thrilling one that has ever happened!" she said beneath her breath. "At the same time, I must punish the Earl. I must pay him out for his outrageous behaviour towards Mama."

Suddenly she flung her arms high in the air.

'It is fate that is helping me,' she thought, then ran to the window.

The music was still playing, the stars were shining, and she knew that the Earl would be searching for her in the garden next door.

She thought he might be angry, and she smiled at the thought of his discomfort.

Then with a sigh of sheer happiness she knew that for one night, at any rate, one of her dreams had come true.

Chapter Four

The next morning, Odetta was certain she had dreamt the whole evening.

Yet, when she awoke, there was the little black mask on her dressing-table, and the blue gown hanging in her wardrobe needed pressing.

She lay for a long while thinking what an enchantment the whole evening had been and how fantastic it was that the Earl was somebody she knew about, and who had been unkind and unnecessarily crushing to her beloved mother.

"I always meant to pay him out somehow for his behaviour," she told herself, "and now is my opportunity."

At the same time she could not help remembering the strange feeling she had when he held her hand, and how exciting it had been to duel with him in words and to feel she was really playing a part in one of her dreams.

When she went downstairs to breakfast in the Morning-Room where the Walmer family ate alone, there was only Lord Walmer there. She had already learnt that Penelope was still asleep.

"Good-morning, Odetta!" he said gravely. "I thought

you would be the only person to keep me company, since last night you enjoyed your beauty-sleep as neither my wife nor my daughter were able to do."

"I suspected they would sleep late, My Lord," Odetta replied.

"I came home early," Lord Walmer announced, "but not as early as I would have liked."

Odetta thought he looked a little tired, and, as he helped himself from one of the silver dishes laid out English fashion on the side-board, he said:

"I find these late nights extremely exhausting, especially as I have so much work to do in the daytime."

"How long do you think you will be staying in Paris?" Odetta asked.

"No longer than I can help," Lord Walmer replied, which told her nothing of what she wanted to know.

When Penelope awoke she was full of complaints as to how boring the party had been.

"Two strangers danced with me," she said, "but most of the time I was left with one of Step-Mama's French friends who talked and talked to me about people I had never heard of and were not the least interesting."

Odetta thought that she would have found it rather amusing, then she remembered how she had enjoyed every moment of the evening even though she had been frightened at her own audacity.

There were more fittings during the day, but every moment she could spare Odetta was frantically altering a gown that she could wear that evening.

She told herself a hundred times that she had no intention of going and that the Earl would wait for her in vain.

Then she was certain that she must see him again if only to make sure that her idea of revenge would be effective.

After what he had said to her last night, after the way

he had flirted with her—at the same time with a sincerity which made her feel that perhaps it was more than a flirtation—she knew that nothing would be more effective than to engage his affections and then disappear.

Considering his rank and that even wearing a mask he was an extremely attractive man, it seemed very odd that he would be really captivated by a stranger whom he had met at a Ball and whom he believed to be a married woman.

But because it seemed part of her dreams, Odetta wanted to believe that he actually did find her alluring, and it would certainly be part of a fairy-story if all day he was looking forward to seeing her again.

"I will see him once again," she told herself, "and if he is as ardent as he was last night, then I can disappear and know that he will feel frustrated and perhaps even angry that I did not find him as attractive as he thinks he is."

At the same time, she had an uncomfortable feeling that she was making excuses for her own behaviour.

But she refused to listen to her conscience and sewed away industriously, transforming another of Lady Walmer's expensive Bond Street gowns into an imitation of a Worth creation.

Because she was in a hurry, she continued to work on a gown she had already started to alter, but when she had nearly finished it she thought it was really too grand for a quiet dinner alone with a Gentleman.

Emelene had told her that Lady Walmer had worn it at a State Ball at Windsor Castle.

Yet, because the material was of light gauze, it was easier to alter than some of the other gowns which were heavy satin or brocade.

"I think it is very kind of you to do this for Emelene," Penelope said as Odetta worked.

"It means a lot to her to be able to sell your Step-

Mama's gowns when she has finished with them," Odetta replied.

"It would be much more sensible if she gave them to you," Penelope said. "You know you could have mine, but as they would be much too short, I do not see how you could change them."

"That is sweet of you," Odetta replied, "but I have no need for such grand gowns."

"When I am married to Simon," Penelope said, "you can come and stay with me, and I will find you a husband just as fascinating as he is."

Odetta smiled to herself, for although she liked Simon and thought him a very worthy young man, the last description she would give him was "fascinating."

Inevitably she found herself thinking of the Earl and the vibrations she had felt coming from him when he was close to her and the way they had sparred with each other in words.

'I shall see him again tonight,' she thought, and felt her heart leap at the idea.

At the same time, when Penelope had gone, protesting that she had no wish to do so, to the Palace with her father and Stepmother, Odetta began to change from the simple home-made gown she was wearing into the silver gauze that was still in some places only tacked.

Emelene, profuse in her thanks, had tidied up Lady Walmer's room with lightning speed and then had left the Embassy to join her friends.

Therefore, Odetta was not afraid of being interrupted as she put on the silver gown and arranged her hair in the most fashionable manner she could manage.

She remembered that the Earl had thought she was English, and when she looked at herself in the mirror she wondered if he would really be deceived into believing she was French.

In her day-dreams she had assumed the part of a French *Princesse*, but now she thought she would have been wiser not to have changed her nationality, or at least to have said that she was Swedish.

Her hair was fair, her skin was so clear that it was very unlike any Frenchwoman's, and although her eyes were grey and not blue, they certainly had nothing Gallic about them.

Then she told hrself it was of no consequence. Whatever the Earl thought about her, they would not meet again after tonight.

When finally she was ready, she picked up the silver scarf that went with the gown and thought that apart from the fact that she was wearing no jewellery, she looked more suitably dressed for a Ball such as last night's than for a quiet *tête-à-tête*.

Yet, in a way it was even more exciting, because she had never dined alone with any man except her father, and actually she had had very few conversations with any man who was not old or married or interested only in parochial matters.

As she slipped her mother's wedding-ring onto her finger, she said as if she thought her mother could hear:

"Forgive me, Mama, if I am doing anything wrong, but it is so exciting to be in Paris, and if I just sit alone in the Embassy I might just as well be at home at the Vicarage."

She had the feeling that her mother would understand, and she added:

"In a way it is not as reprehensible as it might be, because the Earl is a relation, and if I can make him unhappy even for a few hours, then I shall feel he has received his just deserts."

She was not so certain that her mother would have approved of this plan, but nevertheless, as always when she talked to her, she felt that she was near and that her love would prevent her from coming to any harm.

Then with a change of mood that brought a little mocking smile to her lips, Odetta curtseyed to her reflection in the mirror, saying as she did so:

"*Voilà, Madame la Princesse,* go and do your worst, and hope that the Earl suffers in consequence!"

Once again there was the frightening moment of escaping from the house without being seen, but during the day Odetta had found that there was another staircase, by which she could reach the garden without going through the main Hall.

It was not yet dark but the sun had set, and, keeping close to the trees in case anyone should see her from the window, Odetta hurried as swiftly as she could towards a gate that led into the road at the back of the Embassy.

Only as she reached it did she have a sudden moment of panic in case she should find it locked and no key with which to open it.

However, the door was secured inside by two heavy bolts, and she found that if they were pulled back it was possible to open the door easily both from inside the garden and from outside when she wished to return.

She could only pray that no officious servant would push back the bolts in her absence.

Then she was out in the road, looking first to right then to the left for the carriage that should be waiting for her.

It was with a sense of relief that she saw there was one. It was some way to the left, and she realised that the Earl had not suspected last night that she came from the Embassy.

She moved quickly towards the carriage, and only when she reached it did a footman jump down from the box to open the door for her, and she found the Earl sitting inside.

He put out his hand to help her in, and once again she felt a strange sensation when he touched her.

"You have come!" he said in his deep voice, and she knew he was glad to see her.

As she sat down beside him on the comfortable padded seat, he said:

"I behaved in the way I felt you would wish me to by not waiting for you on the pavement in case I should be seen, and not spying to see from which house you emerged."

Odetta thought the cynical note was back in his voice. At the same time, it was somehow different from the way he had first spoken to her yesterday evening.

"Thank you," she said simply.

"Last night I could not see your face," the Earl said, "but now without your mask I can see what you look like."

This was true, Odetta thought, but at the same time she realised that now she too could see him.

She had not looked at him as she stepped into the carriage, because she felt embarrassed, and because it swept over her even more strongly than before how shocked Lord and Lady Walmer would be if they ever found out what she was doing.

But now she raised her eyes to the Earl's face and saw that without his mask he was even better-looking than she had thought he would be.

Yet he definitely had a cynical expression, and his eyes were looking at her in a penetrating way, while at the same time there was something slightly raffish about him.

'He looks like a Buccaneer,' she thought, then substituted the word "Rake" and knew she should not have come.

"You are very lovely," the Earl said, "just as I knew you would be! How did you find Venus when you returned home last night? Or were you swept up by some mystical power into a star?"

"I know I must have seemed rather . . . rude in leaving without saying . . . good-bye," Odetta replied, "but it was very late . . . and I could not . . . stay any . . . longer."

"So to make sure I did not know where you were going, you disposed of me very successfully."

Odetta did not answer. She merely looked away from him with a faint smile on her lips.

"I suspected it was what you might do," the Earl went on. "At the same time, because you are being so mysterious, I find it both frustrating and intriguing."

There was no reply, and after a moment he added:

"I suppose you are aware, Odetta, that you are driving me mad?"

"I think that is very unlikely, *Milord*, but if I am, then you must put it down to the magic of Paris."

"Do you really think you personify Paris?" the Earl enquired. "Now that I see you without your mask, I do not believe for one moment that you are French."

Odetta stiffened. In her dream-world she was sure *Princesse* de Charleval would certainly consider that an insult.

"If you are going to be rude to me, *Monsieur*," she said, "then I think I would be wise to dine elsewhere."

The Earl laughed.

"Do you really think I would let you escape me when I have been afraid all day that you would have returned to the firmament above us and were, after all, immortal?"

Odetta thought with satisfaction that that was exactly what she wanted him to feel.

But there was no time to say more, for they had arrived at a Restaurant which Odetta could see was situated in a small Square.

There were several tables and chairs outside, which must have been used in the daytime, but there was nobody sitting there now, and when they entered she saw that the Restaurant was very small and consisted of only two rooms.

There were sofas for the diners, a profusion of flowers, and a few pictures on the walls, obviously by modern artists.

Odetta looked round her with delight. It was exactly what she had thought a French Restaurant would be like, but she had been quite certain she would never be lucky enough to eat in one.

"I want to talk to you," the Earl said, "and that is why I have brought you here."

They were shown to a table in a corner of the smaller room, and when they were seated he said:

"Is there anything you particularly fancy, or would you like me to order for you?"

"I am ready to believe that your choice will be good," Odetta replied.

"As the French are certain of the inferiority of English food, I consider that a compliment," he replied.

He had a long conversation with the *maître d'Hôtel*, and the *Sommelier* before finally he sat back to look at Odetta with a smile on his lips.

She knew that his eyes were taking in the expensive elegance of her gown, and she was not really surprised when he said:

"There is no need for me to tell you that you look like the star from which you have come, but I am rather surprised that, unlike most Frenchwomen, you have omitted to glitter."

His eyes were on her neck, and although she knew he was referring to the fact that she was not wearing a necklace, there was something in his expression which made her blush.

Then, before she could answer him, he said:

"But you are right. Your skin is perfect, and it would be a mistake to wear diamonds which would conceal it."

It was difficult for Odetta to find her voice, and when she did she said:

"I came here tonight, *Monsieur*, to enjoy your conversation. Let us forget the compliments which last night we decided were the prerogative of the French."

"But those made by an Englishman are sincere," the Earl said, "and when I tell you that you are very lovely and shine like a star, I am speaking the truth."

Odetta turned her face away from him.

Then she told herself that if she was really the *Princesse* she was pretending to be, she would not behave like an embarrassed School-girl who had never had a compliment paid to her before.

"As we are being so personal," she said after a moment, "shall I tell you that without your mask you look like a Buccaneer."

The Earl smiled.

"I believe one of my ancestors was quite a famous pirate in the reign of Queen Elizabeth, and perhaps what I should do is to kidnap you and carry you away in my ship to some far-off land where nobody will ever find us."

Odetta forced herself to give a little laugh.

"I am sure, *Milord*, that after the first excitement of snatching me away, you would find it very boring to have to confine yourself to one woman, when no doubt your interest both in France and England ranges over a number."

The Earl laughed.

"Now you are making me out to be 'Blue Beard,' and if we are still talking of fairy-stories, I would like to point out that Cinderella left her glass slipper behind when she disappeared, but there was no sign of your handkerchief."

"But you did not have to search for me. I am here, as I promised you I would be."

"Suppose after tonight you disappear?" the Earl insisted. "Where shall I look for you?"

Odetta made a gesture with her hands.

"Questions! Always questions!" she said. "I did not come out to dinner, *Monsieur,* to be interrogated."

"Why should you be so mysterious?" the Earl asked angrily. "You know that I want to see you every minute that it is possible to do so, yet because you are so elusive you are making me apprehensive."

"I have a feeling," Odetta said slowly, "that in the past the Earl of Houghton has had everything he wanted far too easily, and it will be very good for his soul to be a little unsure of his own powers."

"Now you are being deliberately provocative," the Earl said. "How do you know I have everything I want in life? What do you know about me?"

"Nothing," Odetta replied ingenuously, "except that I have always been told that English noblemen were of great importance in their own country. The way you walk and hold yourself tells me that you are a man who has never faced adversity or defeat."

"That is true," the Earl said, "and that is why, my lovely little *Princesse,* I do not intend to lose the battle where you are concerned."

"Has there to be a battle, *Monsieur?*"

She expected him to answer quickly, but instead he said slowly:

"I have the uncomfortable feeling that you are laughing at me. I feel too that you are not what you pretend to be, and there is also something else I do not understand."

Odetta clapped her hands together.

"That is excellent, *Monsieur.* I have you guessing . . . as you say in English . . . and that will make it difficult for you to forget me."

"Why should there be any chance of my forgetting you?" the Earl asked sharply.

He paused before he went on:

"Look at me, Odetta! I want to know what devilment you are up to."

Odetta raised her eye-brows.

"Why should you imagine I am up to any 'devilment' as you call it?"

"Because you are deliberately making me anxious, or, if you prefer it, you are frightening me!"

There was silence for a moment. Then he said quietly:

"I told you to look at me!"

Because he commanded her, and also because it was hard to resist him when he spoke in that particular tone of voice, Odetta turned her head slowly.

She was very near to him and she found herself looking into his eyes, which were the dark, turbulent blue of the sea, and it was impossible to look away.

Perhaps it was a minute, or perhaps a few centuries passed before the Earl said:

"When I spoke to you last night, I was hoping against hope to find some sort of amusement at the Ball. Then you know as well as I do that it became not a question of amusement but something very different."

"I . . . I do not know what you . . . mean."

"You do know, because you feel just as I do," the Earl said. "We met, Odetta, and it was not just a meeting of strangers, but of two people who were reunited by fate."

Because of the way he was speaking, Odetta felt herself quiver.

She felt too as if he mesmerised her, and she had a feeling that there was nothing in the world but his eyes and the closeness of him.

Then with a superhuman effort she broke the spell that held her and said in a voice that did not sound like her own:

"You are . . . frightening me."

"In what way?"

"You are making something that was meant to be light and amusing . . . serious and . . . overwhelming."

"That is what it is," the Earl said, "and you cannot escape, Odetta, any more than I can."

"That is . . . not true," Odetta tried to say, but the words seemed to stick in her throat.

Almost without her realising it, the hours seemed to speed by, and while she talked to the Earl, or rather tried to parry his suspicions, she felt all the time as if they were speaking to each other without words, and there was no reason to say anything.

When the Earl paid the bill and they went outside to where the carriage was waiting, she thought that the evening was over and now she must leave him and they would never meet again. But at the same time she wanted to stay a little longer.

She wanted to postpone the inevitable, even though she knew there was no point in doing so.

As they drove away from the Restaurant, the Earl did not speak. He merely sat back in the corner of the carriage, and as a street-light occasionally illuminated his face, Odetta thought he looked stern and even a little grim.

She tried to think of something to say, something that he would remember after they were parted. But her mind was a blank, and all she could be aware of was a strange feeling in her body because he was close to her.

Then as she thought they must have reached the road at the back of the Embassy she realised that the horses were travelling up the Champs Élysées.

She looked towards the Earl for an explanation, and spoke for the first time since they had left the Restaurant.

"Where are you taking me?"

"There is something I want to show you," he replied, then once again lapsed into silence.

They drove on, and when at last the horses came to a standstill Odetta realised they were in the Bois.

There were trees on either side of the road, and as the footman got down to open the carriage-door, she knew that the Earl intended them to alight.

He stepped out first and helped her to the ground, which was dry from the sun and soft with the moss which grew beneath the trees.

He took her arm and led her under the branches, following a small path.

However, it was easy to find the way because of the stars overhead and a half-moon climbing up the sky whose light turned the world to silver.

They walked on until the path turned, and there in front of them was a cascade falling with a musical sound into a pool filled with water-lilies and edged with flowers.

The moonlight on the water, which shimmered almost dazzlingly with its movements, was very lovely, and because the light came from above, Odetta instinctively turned her face up to the sky to look at the moon surrounded by stars.

As she did so, the Earl put his arms round her to hold her close to him. In a split second she knew what he intended, and she was not really startled because it was in her dream.

Then as his lips found hers, it seemed part of the sound of the falling water, the light of the moon, and the glitter of the stars overhead.

His arms tightened. As he drew her closer and still closer, she felt something warm and wonderful move slowly up through her heart and breasts, into her throat, until it touched her lips and became not only hers but his.

She knew that this was what she had yearned for and wanted, not only since she had met the Earl but long

before, when in her fairy-stories the Prince had personified
the love she sought but thought she might never find.

Now it was love that the Earl drew from between her
lips, and love which made her heart beat against his.

Love that filled the night and made her feel as if they
both were flying to the moon.

She knew this was the ecstasy and rapture of love,
which before had only been words but now was a part of
herself, and she was dazzled and bemused by it until she
could no longer think but only feel.

The Earl's lips became more insistent and demanding,
until Odetta felt a little flicker of fire move within her
which was different from anything she had felt before.

It was like a flame leaping in the dark, and yet making a
light that was magical and at the same time wildly exciting.

Because in a way it made her afraid, as the Earl raised
his head, she could only give a little murmur and hide
her face against his neck.

"My sweet, my darling!" he said, and his voice was
unsteady. "How could either of us fight against this?"

The passion in his voice made Odetta quiver but not
with fear.

Then he put his fingers under her chin and turned her
face up to his to look down into her eyes, which seemed
to hold the stars in their depths.

"You are beautiful!" he said. "But what I feel for you is
so much more than mere beauty. You are mine and I can
never lose you!"

Then he was kissing her again, kissing her with long,
slow, passionate kisses which made Odetta feel that she
no longer existed but was his, as he had said she was, and
she had no identity of her own.

A long time later, it might have been an hour or a
century of time, they were driving back the way they
had come, and now Odetta was close in the Earl's arms,
and her head was on his shoulder.

They did not speak, for there was no need for words.

They were close in a way that was indescribable, no longer two people but one.

Then when the horses came to a stop in the same place where the Earl had waited for her, Odetta moved.

It was impossible to explain how it hurt her physically to do so, as if she were cutting away a part of herself that now belonged to him.

"I cannot bear you to leave me," he said, and his voice sounded raw. "When shall I see you again?"

It was then that Odetta woke up to reality, and she knew that ever since dinner she had forgotten everything: who she was, what she had intended, and where she had to return.

For a moment her head felt as though it was filled with stars and it was impossible to come down to earth and think clearly of anything except a happiness that seemed to pulsate through her.

Then she said in a voice that was almost incoherent:

"I . . . I m-must . . . go!"

"I understand, my precious," the Earl said, "but before you do so, you must tell me when I can see you again. Will you have luncheon with me?"

The mere question, simple though it was, made Odetta aware of the complexities, the difficulties in which she had become entangled.

She shook her head, and he said:

"Then you will dine with me again. I have to talk to you, Odetta, you know that."

As if she had asked the question, he went on:

"About our future—our future together."

"There is . . . no time . . . now," Odetta said quickly.

"Yes, I know," the Earl agreed, "and when we meet tomorrow I will kiss you and you will carry me up to the stars. But we must also try to be sensible, my darling."

Odetta thought that was what she was trying to be, but it was very difficult.

If she carried him up to the stars, she still felt as if the glitter of them made it impossible to think of anything except that his arms were round her and his lips were very near to hers.

"I love . . . you!" she said, and her heart echoed the words.

Then he was kissing her again, kissing her until she thought for one wild moment that she had died from the sheer wonder of it.

"You must go back," the Earl said at length, and she knew it was an effort for him to speak, just as it was for her.

"I would not want you to get into trouble on my behalf," he said gently, "not at the moment, not until we have had a talk together."

Odetta's eyes searched for his in the shadows of the carriage.

"G-good-bye . . ." she said softly.

He took her hand and held it against his cheek.

"Let us say it in French," he said. *"Au revoir,* my precious, beautiful little star. Think of me, dream of me until we are together again."

"Au . . . revoir," Odetta repeated, and it was difficult not to let her voice break on the words.

Then the carriage-door was opened and she was walking away alone, walking at first slowly, then swiftly, until she broke into a run.

She reached the door into the Embassy garden, it opened easily, and when she was inside she pushed back the bolts one by one.

As she did so, she thought she was bolting out love and had lost it forever.

*   *   *

The following morning, after a sleepless night, Odetta told herself that if she suffered it was entirely her own fault and there was nothing she could do about it.

Sleepless, she had turned back the curtains to stare out at the moon and know that the Earl was as far distant from her as were the stars, and if she left him she had no-one to blame but herself.

She remembered her Nanny saying to her when she was a child: 'If you play with fire you'll get burnt,' and that was exactly what she had done.

She had played with fire, and it had turned out to be with a man more dominating than those in her childish dreams. While she had wanted to make him suffer, all she had done was to crucify herself.

"I love him! I love him!" she cried into her pillow, and knew how stupid she had been to let one of her fairy-stories become reality.

She knew there was nothing she could do and it would be humiliating to let the Earl become aware that she was not a *Princesse* who had come to him like a star, but an insignificant girl from a Vicarage who had acted a lie and told lies and finally had given him her heart under false pretences.

How could he ever forgive her for such behaviour?

She could imagine nothing more humiliating than to see the expression of contempt and disdain on his face and to hear him once again speak to her sarcastically and mockingly as he had at first.

When she had hung the beautiful silver gauze gown back in her wardrobe, she had known that the play was over and it would be impossible for her ever to act the same part again.

There was nothing more to say, nothing more to do, except ring down the curtain and go back to being herself.

"I love . . . him!" she whispered.

But she knew that to prove her love she had to disappear—not in order to hurt him and leave him frustrated and unhappy, as she had planned, but because since she loved him she could not bear to see him disillusioned.

That would be worse than anything else.

As it was, he would think of her as the *Princesse*, a married woman, with whom for one brief moment he had been enamoured. She would remain in his mind as someone beautiful, desirable, and as enchanting as the star with which he had compared her.

It would be a very different thing to know that he had been deceived by an English girl who had nothing to recommend her except a capacity for lying.

If he knew that, Odetta was sure it would disillusion not only him but also herself.

Now she knew what real love was like.

Now the feelings that she had imagined in her dreams had become real, and she was aware that they were far more wonderful, more compelling, more enchanting, and more ecstatic than anything she, in her ignorance, could possibly have contemplated.

'So this is love!' she thought.

She knew that never again would she hear the music of a waltz, walk in a garden, dance, or look at the stars without feeling that her heart was calling for the Earl, although he would never be aware of it.

She faced the fact that she would never feel the same for another man; it would be impossible, once she had touched the very peaks of the mountains, to climb any higher.

What was more, if she ever married, which was unlikely, her husband could never be as real to her as the man who had walked straight out of her dreams to take her heart and make it his for eternity.

Because it had been so rapturous and so wonderful,

she could not cry, now that she had lost him, but only feel that in a way she had been blessed and privileged to find love in such an unexpected fashion.

"Now I can go home without a single regret," she told herself. "Paris has given me everything I expected, and so much more."

When she was dressed, she stood at the window looking out into the sunlight, telling herself that she must never, never regret what had happened.

Yet she was aware that already there was a pain in her heart because the day had dawned and there was no chance of seeing the Earl.

He would wait for her in vain, then finally he would drive away.

"He will forget, of course he will forget," she told herself, "but I will remember him forever. He will fill my dreams, but there will be no happy ending."

She was still standing at the window when the door behind her opened with a crash and she turned round quickly.

It was Penelope, in her night-gown, with her hair falling over her shoulders, her eyes shining, and an expression of excitement on her face which Odetta had not seen since they had left England.

"What is it?" she asked.

Penelope shut the door behind her, then before she spoke she ran across the room to be close to Odetta.

"What do you think? Oh, Odetta, what do you think? Simon is in Paris!"

"Simon!" Odetta exclaimed. "But why? How do you know?"

"He left a note for me. One of the maids brought it up and said it had been left by a gentleman at the door, who insisted I be awakened and given it immediately, as it was of such importance."

She made a sound of delight before she went on:

"It was clever of him, because he knew Step-Mama would be asleep and I would not yet have come down to breakfast."

"Why is Simon in Paris?" Odetta enquired.

"He says," Penelope replied, opening the letter she held in her hand, "that he has something of great importance to tell me. He says that he must see me and will call back for a reply within half-an-hour."

She glanced at the clock.

"That means he will be here at eight o'clock, before we go down to breakfast. Oh, Odetta, where can we see him?"

"It is impossible for you to go anywhere alone," Odetta said quickly.

"I know," Penelope agreed, "but you will come with me. We can say we are going to a fitting at Worth's."

"Yes, of course," Odetta replied, "but we shall have to go there in a carriage."

As she spoke, she thought that she could not trust the servants not to relate to one another that she and Penelope had met a man, in which case Emelene might mention it to Lady Walmer.

On the other hand, they might repeat it to Mr. Sheffield, who would doubtless think it his duty to tell Penelope's father.

"I have to see him! I have to see him!" Penelope said insistently.

"Yes, dearest, but we have to be careful," Odetta replied soothingly. "If your father knew that Simon was in Paris, he might think it very strange that he should want to see you, and I am sure your Stepmother would disapprove."

"She disapproves of everything!" Penelope said crossly. "Please, Odetta, think what we can do."

Odetta thought of the Bois.

"We will ask if we can go for a fitting to *Monsieur* Worth," she said, "which of course your Stepmother would expect us to do. Then we will stay only a short time in the Rue de la Paix, and because it is still early we will ask the coachman to take us for a drive in the Bois."

Penelope's eyes lit up.

"Of course!" she exclaimed. "No-one will see us there. But where can we tell Simon to meet us?"

"There is an Aquarium," Odetta replied, "and the coachman will not think it at all strange that we should wish to visit it."

Penelope clapped her hands together.

"You are so clever! It will be easy for Simon to find the Aquarium, and I will tell him to wait for us inside."

She went to the small *secretaire* which stood in the corner of Odetta's bedroom, pulled out a piece of writing-paper embossed with the Britannic coat-of-arms, and quickly wrote a letter.

"Which maid gave you Simon's letter?" Odetta asked when she had finished.

"The young maid—I think she is called Jeanne."

"Oh yes, I know which one," Odetta said. "I expect Simon bribed her, and perhaps we should do the same thing."

"How much shall we give her?" Penelope asked.

"Not too much," Odetta said. "She might boast about it."

They finally decided that two francs would be the right amount, and Odetta rang the bell.

As she expected, Jeanne answered it.

"I understand, Jeanne, you have been very kind in bringing *Mademoiselle* Penelope a letter," Odetta said, "and there is somebody coming back in a short while to receive her reply. Will you please give this to the gentleman? And here is a small *pourboire* for your trouble."

The maid bobbed a curtsey.

"Merci beaucoup, M'mselle!"

"And, Jeanne," Odetta went on, "there may be further

messages for *Mademoiselle*, and I would be very grateful
if you would not mention it to anyone that you have
carried them to her."

"*Non, non, M'mselle*, I would not speak of it, that I
promise you!"

Jeanne gave them a very understanding smile, and
when she had gone from the room, Odetta laughed.

"I have always heard that in France they understand
love," she remarked.

Even as she spoke, she felt she wanted to add:

"And Englishmen understand it too."

But she knew that that was something she had to forget.

Chapter Five

As the horses reached the Bois, Odetta found herself overwhelmed by her memories of what had happened the night before.

For the moment she felt as if she were once again walking under the trees with the Earl beside her. Then when they reached the cascade . . .

She forced herself to stop thinking and to say somewhat incoherently to Penelope:

"It is . . . such a . . . lovely day . . . and the Bois is so . . . beautiful!"

Even as she spoke, she realised that Penelope was not listening to her, and she thought that once one was in love it was impossible to think of anything but the person one loved.

They drew up outside the Aquarium, and because Penelope was in such a hurry to jump out of the carriage, Odetta put a warning hand on her arm.

They walked in through the entrance and across a small vestibule, then found themselves in a wide corridor plunged in shadow.

Odetta with a quick glance saw a series of pictures lit

by the light of a Blue Grotto which gave them a very magical effect.

Then the next moment she heard Penelope give a little cry as a man came from the shadows towards them. It was Simon Johnson.

Odetta had only seen him dressed in country clothes before, and she thought now he looked different and very much more presentable.

But there was no doubt that to Penelope the only thing that mattered was that he was there. Her hands were in his and her words were tumbling over themselves as she exclaimed:

"Simon! It is really you! I have wanted so much to see you!"

"And I to see you," he said in a voice that was very deep and sincere.

"But why? Why are you here?" Penelope asked.

As if Simon realised they had forgotten everything but themselves, he disentangled his hand and, holding it out to Odetta, said:

"Thank you for coming with Penelope. I am sure it was you who thought of the Aquarium."

Odetta smiled.

"It was," she admitted, "and it appears to be a very convenient place in which to hide."

Simon glanced round.

"Let us go somewhere where there will be fewer people," he said. "I have something important to tell Penelope."

Penelope slipped her hand into his and they walked down the corridor, while Odetta looked curiously at the chambers that had been made in the thickness of the walls.

She had never seen an Aquarium before and she was fascinated to observe that there was a bed of sand in the bottom of each fish-pool, stones and fragments of rocks partially covered with plants, while sea-scapes had been painted to make each cavern picturesque and very attractive.

She longed to ask the Earl if he had been here, then was certain he would not be interested, but her imagination was telling her that she was seeing the mountains and valleys of an unknown country or of what might even be a new planet.

They reached the end of the corridor where there was a wooden seat for visitors, which fortunately was empty.

Simon and Penelope sat down on it and Odetta was about to join them when she thought it would be tactless.

"Shall I leave you?" she asked. "I am quite happy to look at the fish."

She would have moved away, but Simon said quickly:

"No, please stay. I feel we may need your help."

Curious as to what he was about to impart, Odetta sat down.

"Nothing is wrong?" Penelope asked quickly, and Simon put out his hand protectively to take hers.

"No, darling," he replied. "I have come here to ask you to marry me as quickly as possible."

Penelope gave an inarticulate little cry, and his fingers tightened on hers as he said:

"You knew before you left that I wanted to marry you, but it was very difficult to know how we could do so and, if we took the law into our own hands and ran away, what we would live on. Now all that has changed."

"In what way?" Penelope asked.

"My uncle has died," Simon explained. "He was my father's brother, but he never married and was comparatively well off."

He smiled before he said:

"Perhaps not by your father's standards, but because I am his Godson and he thought my father would look after my two brothers, he has left me his house and Estate in Huntingdonshire, where he had a large farm."

He looked into Penelope's eyes, raised adoringly to his, and asked:

"Would you be content to be a farmer's wife?"

"You know I would!" Penelope cried. "Oh, Simon, does this really mean we can be married?"

"As far as I am concerned, I would marry you today or tomorrow, so that you can help me take over my new property and start supervising the farm, which will be very exciting for me."

"And for me too!" Penelope exclaimed. "Oh, Simon, do you think Papa will let me marry you now?"

"That is something I intend to ask him today."

"Today?" Penelope echoed in astonishment, and Odetta was also surprised.

"I see no point in waiting," Simon said.

"And if he refuses?" Penelope asked in a low voice.

"Then I am going to ask you if you love me enough to run away with me!"

Odetta saw by the expression on Simon's face how much Penelope mattered to him.

After just the slightest pause Penelope said:

"Yes, of course! I will do—anything you—want. I love you and I could—never be happy with—anybody else."

"That is what I hoped and prayed you would say," Simon said.

Odetta saw him tighten his hold on Penelope's hands until her fingers turned white.

Then as they looked into each other's eyes, forgetting everything and everybody except themselves, Odetta rose to move a little way from them and occupy herself in looking at the fish.

Simon and Penelope were lost in a world of their own and it was nearly half-an-hour later when Odetta saw them waving to her and walked back to join them.

"Help us, Odetta!" Penelope cried impulsively. "You will have to help us!"

"Of course I will do that," Odetta answered, "but perhaps your father will agree to what Simon has asked and there will be no difficulties."

"I hope so," Penelope answered.

She did not sound very confident, and Odetta was certain that however much Simon Johnson now owned, Lord Walmer would not consider him a suitable husband for his only child.

However, there was no point in anticipating the worst, and as they talked, going over every detail again and again, Odetta tried to be optimistic and give them hope.

"When do you think I should be able to speak to His Lordship?" Simon asked Odetta.

"I do not know exactly what his plans are," she replied, "but when he finished breakfast he picked up a brief-case which was left on a chair, and there was also a pile of papers with it."

"That sounds as if he might be working in the Embassy."

"Then let us go back! Let us go back at once!" Penelope cried. "I do not think I could bear the suspense of waiting for hours until we know what Papa will say."

"I think it would be wise if I did not go with you but went alone," Simon said. "What I suggest you do is let me leave immediately. I have a hackney-carriage waiting for me, and I will go on ahead. When you reach the Embassy, if His Lordship is there, as I hope he will be, I shall doubtless be with him and you can join us."

He paused before he said:

"On the other hand, if I have left, it will mean I have been refused. In which case we must arrange where we can meet."

"Oh, Simon, I shall be praying very, very hard that father will say 'yes,'" Penelope said.

Simon looked at Odetta.

"Do you think there is a chance for me, Miss Charlwood?"

Odetta hesitated.

She wanted to encourage him, but at the same time she felt it would perhaps be kinder for him to know what she really thought.

However, there was no need for words, for Simon knew by the expression on her face what she was thinking, and he said quickly:

"Very well. We will make our plans, and this is what I want you both to do. . . ."

Odetta found he had arranged everything in his own mind, and she thought that his unexpected inheritance had given him a determination that he had never had before.

Or perhaps because he was in love it gave him an objective that was too precious to lose.

When he had left them, Penelope watched him walk firmly away down the shadowy corridor, and only when he was out of sight did she turn to Odetta with a little cry.

"Oh, Odetta, help me!" she begged. "I love him and I cannot lose him now!"

"I do not think you will do that, whatever happens," Odetta answered.

"I feel sure Papa will not agree to my marrying him, and Step-Mama is so snobby she would turn up her nose at the Johnsons."

"If that happens, then you will have to be very brave and do as Simon suggests," Odetta said.

She knew that most people would think it very reprehensible of her to encourage Penelope to run away with anyone, least of all a man whom her father considered socially beneath him.

But, knowing Penelope so well, she knew that she would never be happy with anyone she did not love, and whatever Lady Walmer might think, it would not be easy to find her a husband.

Moreover, like all rather simple people, Penelope could

be very obstinate, and if she was not allowed to marry Simon, Odetta was sure she would make herself unpleasant to any other man who approached her.

What was more, without looks, a large fortune, or outstanding talent, and with a dislike of everything social, it was going to be difficult even for Lady Walmer to find a man who would ask Penelope to marry him.

"She will be happy with Simon," Odetta told herself firmly, and knew that whatever the repercussions on herself, she would help them both to the very best of her ability.

She drove back to the Embassy with Penelope, who was in such a state of agitation that she had great difficulty in keeping her calm.

"If your father says he will not agree to your marriage, you will only make things worse if you make a scene," she said. "So please, Penelope, say as little as possible."

"Why should Papa have been allowed to marry whom he liked, while I have to obey him?" Penelope asked. "I have to marry Simon—I have to!"

"You will marry him," Odetta said quietly, "but if it really becomes a case of having to run away, your father might, if you appear to be too upset, make things very difficult."

This was the threat which made Penelope pull herself together. Although she was very pale and Odetta knew she was trembling when they reached the Embassy, she stepped out of the carriage with some dignity.

They walked into the Hall, and because Odetta knew it was impossible for Penelope to speak, she asked:

"Is Lord Walmer here?"

"*Oui, M'mselle*," a flunkey replied. "His Lordship is in the *Antichambre*."

Odetta glanced at Penelope, realised she now had strict control over herself, and questioned:

"His Lordship is alone?"

"There was a gentleman with him, but I think he has left."

Penelope made a little murmur, and Odetta quickly put her hand in hers to draw her across the Hall towards the Antechamber.

A footman opened the door and they went in to find Lord Walmer sitting at a desk, a large stack of papers in front of him.

He glanced up, saw his daughter, and rose to his feet.

"I was just about to send for you, Penelope," he said, "but now that you are here, I have something to say to you."

Odetta gave Penelope a little push so that she moved towards her father, while she herself stood back.

Lord Walmer walked purposefully towards the fireplace to stand with his back to it.

When Penelope reached the centre of the room she stood staring at her father, her fingers clasped tightly together.

Lord Walmer cleared his throat.

"As you are doubtless aware," he said, "a young man called Simon Johnson, the son of a neighbouring farmer at home, has called to inform me that he wishes to marry you."

Odetta heard Penelope draw in her breath, but she did not speak, and after a moment, as if he had expected her to, Lord Walmer went on:

"I have told him firmly, so that there can be no possible misunderstanding, that I consider his request an impertinence. I would not in any circumstances countenance your marriage to a man who is not our social equal, and I have made it clear to him, as I do now to you, that you are not to see each other again!"

Almost before Lord Walmer had finished the sentence, Penelope gave a little scream like that of a small animal that had been caught in a trap.

Then she turned and ran back towards the door, passing Odetta as she did so. She pulled it open and went out and they could hear her footsteps running across the Hall towards the staircase.

Lord Walmer looked at Odetta and he was frowning.

"I suppose you were aware that she has been seeing this fellow?" he asked.

"I was not aware of it until just before we left England, My Lord."

"You will kindly see that there is no further communication between them," Lord Walmer said. "I consider it very undesirable that my daughter should in any way associate with someone of that sort, and when we return home I shall take steps to see that it does not occur again."

Odetta did not reply and he added sharply:

"You will carry out my orders, and, what is more, you will intercept any letters that Johnson may send her or that she may try to send him."

Odetta curtseyed but she made no answer to Lord Walmer, and as she turned towards the door she heard him make an exasperated sound before he ejaculated:

"Dammit all, I do not know what the world is coming to when upstart farmers think they can marry into my family!"

Odetta closed the door quietly and ran to join Penelope.

She was in her bedroom, looking very white and shaken, and when Odetta joined her she flung her arms round her neck and burst into tears.

"Do not cry," Odetta said. "You must have known that your father would not agree to such a marriage."

"He will—try to stop us—whatever Simon may— do."

"I am sure of that," Odetta said, "and that is why we must act quickly. Are you prepared, as you said you were, to marry Simon without your father's approval?"

Penelope controlled her tears.

"You—know I am!" she said. "It is only rather—frightening to leave Papa—and I always thought he—loved me."

"I am sure he does," Odetta said. "It is just that he is very proud, and like all parents he wants the best for his child."

"Simon *is* the best," Penelope said fiercely.

"Yes, he is," Odetta agreed.

Penelope wiped her tears away before she said:

"Tell him! Tell Simon at once, Odetta, that I am willing to marry him and I think we should do it quickly."

"That is exactly what I have been thinking," Odetta said. "I may be wrong, but I have the idea that your father will insist on having somebody older than me to chaperone you and escort you when you go out shopping."

Penelope gave a cry of terror.

"He will do that so that I . . . cannot see Simon? Oh, Odetta, tell Simon that we must run away now—today!"

"You are quite sure that is what you want?"

Penelope nodded her head and now she was smiling.

"Quite, quite sure!"

Afterwards, Odetta wondered how everything could have gone so smoothly.

They had arranged for Jeanne to take a note to Simon, who was waiting for it.

His plan, which he had outlined to them in the Aquarium, went into operation like a well-greased machine, and there were no difficulties or last-minute hitches to prevent them from being married.

Simon had discovered as soon as he arrived in Paris that it was easy for them to have a Civil Marriage as long as they could vouch for being over the age of consent.

He had also been told that there were always "shady" Solicitors hanging round the Mayor's offices who would provide Birth Certificates in place of those that had

conveniently been "lost," on the payment of a large fee
for their services.

Penelope's Birth Certificate therefore showed her to be
twenty-one, and Odetta watched them joined together
by a few words in front of a flamboyantly dressed official
who, when the ceremony was over, kissed them both on
the cheek.

Then, carefully carrying the document which made them
man and wife, they walked out to the carriage that was to
carry them to the Gare du Nord.

It was impossible for Penelope to take a lot of luggage
with her, but, as she had said to Odetta:

"You can bring everything back to England with you,
and if you pretend that my new gowns are yours, Papa
will not confiscate them."

However, Odetta had cleverly modified Simon's origi-
nal plan so that Penelope in fact was able to take several
of her new evening-gowns with her and enough afternoon-
gowns to make her look attractive on her honeymoon.

When Penelope received Simon's note, in reply to
hers, saying that he would pick them up at No. 7 Rue de
la Paix at two-thirty, Odetta had sent a message downstairs to say that Miss Penelope was indisposed.

She knew a luncheon-party had been arranged at which
the Ambassador would be present, and she thought it
unlikely that Lord and Lady Walmer would, in the circumstances, insist on Penelope's presence.

Therefore, food was brought up to the bedroom for
both Penelope and Odetta, and they snatched mouthfuls
from the trays while they feverishly packed all they could
into the smallest of her cases, which would not arouse
suspicion when the servants carried them downstairs.

They waited until they knew the luncheon would be
well underway. Then Odetta rang for Jeanne and told her
that *Mademoiselle* Penelope had remembered she had a

very important fitting with *Monsieur* Worth at two o'clock.

"It was the only time he could squeeze her in," Odetta said most convincingly, "and as she wants several of her gowns altered, we are taking them with us, and we must not be late or it will be impossible for him to see her."

If Jeanne was suspicious she did not say so, and Odetta knew she would make the same explanation to the footman who was sent to order a carriage from the stables.

They hurried downstairs, knowing that as the luncheon was taking place in the *Grand Salle à manger* they would not be seen.

Nevertheless, both Penelope and Odetta held their breath until the carriage drove out of the courtyard and they were in the Rue du Faubourg St. Honoré.

When they arrived with their cases at No. 7 Rue de la Paix, Odetta told the coachman to come back in two-and-a-half hours.

"We shall be here at least that length of time," she said, "and there is no point in your keeping the horses waiting in the street."

The coachmen were pleased, as she knew they would be, and they touched their high cockaded hats and drove away, while Odetta told *Monsieur* Worth's servants to leave the suitcases in the Hall.

There was still half-an-hour before Simon was due to arrive, and Penelope was delighted to find that two of the new gowns that she had ordered were actually ready for her.

To pack them they needed another case, and when they were all put inside the *voiture*, there was hardly room for Odetta.

However, she squeezed herself in, saying:

"I think it would be best if I come with you to the Station, then return to the Embassy in this carriage."

"Yes, of course," Simon agreed, "although really we should drop you off first."

Penelope gave a little cry of protest.

"That could be dangerous! Papa might see me!"

"I have thought of that," Simon replied, "and I am sure Miss Charlwood will not mind driving back from the Station alone, even though it may be unconventional."

Odetta laughed.

"Not half as unconventional as what you two are doing!" she replied. "But I am not looking forward to the fuss there will be when they find you gone."

"Please, please, keep Papa from knowing for as long as possible," Penelope begged. "Suppose he reaches Calais before we get there and is waiting to snatch me away from Simon before we can cross the Channel?"

"It would be impossible for him to do so," Simon replied firmly, "unless he flies like a bird!"

The carriage, piled with the luggage, reached La Mairie and when they came out again Penelope was so happy to be Simon's wife that no other problems or difficulties seemed to cross her mind.

They drove almost in silence to the Gare du Nord, Penelope looking adoringly at her husband and he at her, and only when they were about to leave did she put her arms round Odetta and say:

"Thank you, thank you, dearest Odetta, and when you get home you must be the first visitor that we have in Huntingdonshire. I want to show you what a good farmer's wife I shall make."

Odetta kissed her affectionately and stood on the platform watching until the train was out of sight.

Then, straightening her shoulders, she told herself that now she had to face the music.

She drove back to the Embassy, and as she went she was thinking not of Penelope and Simon but of the Earl.

She had the feeling that he would be thinking of her, and that perhaps he was finding that time was passing slowly until they could meet as he thought they had arranged to do.

For a moment she was tempted to go to him, tell him who she was, and ask him if what he felt for her last night was strong enough to make him forgive her deception.

Then she thought unhappily that it would be tantamount to asking him if he would marry her, and she knew the answer to that without hearing him say it.

She was quite certain that if the Earl was not married already, he had no intention of giving up his freedom for any woman, least of all for one he would consider his social inferior, just as Lord Walmer thought of Simon Johnson.

She could imagine nothing more humiliating or embarrassing than that he should have to try to explain that mariage was not and never had been his intention where she was concerned.

Or perhaps, worse still, he might actually offer her a very different place in his life!

"No, no, it is all over! Finished!" she murmured, and realised as she spoke that the carriage had reached the Embassy.

She walked into the Hall and thought the Butler was looking at her in rather a strange way as he came to her side to say:

"His Lordship enquired for *M'mselle* Penelope about an hour ago, *M'mselle*. When he was informed that you had gone out, he gave orders that you were to join him in the *Antichambre* as soon as you returned."

Odetta drew in her breath.

She knew this was going to be a very unpleasant ordeal and she was not mistaken.

When she went into the Anteroom, both Lord and Lady Walmer were there and she knew by the expressions on their faces that they were expecting Penelope to be with her.

She curtseyed as Lord Walmer asked sharply:

"Where is Penelope? I gave orders I wanted to see both of you!"

"I am afraid, My Lord, that is impossible."

"What do you mean—impossible?"

Odetta found it difficult to answer him, but finally the words came.

"She . . . she has left . . . Paris."

"Left Paris?"

It was Lady Walmer who ejaculated the words, while Lord Walmer stared at Odetta in sheer astonishment.

"She has . . . m-married Simon . . . Johnson!" Odetta said quietly.

"That is impossible!" Lord Walmer thundered. "She is a minor. She has to have my consent."

"Where were they married?" Lady Walmer questioned.

It was then that Odetta faced an interrogation that was to prove more and more unpleasant.

Finally, while Lord Walmer was still shouting at her, Lady Walmer was silent and Odetta was sure that she was thinking with some satisfaction that Penelope was now off her hands and it would suit her best to do nothing about it.

At last Lord Walmer said:

"I consider the part you have played in this disgraceful affair completely unforgivable! You will pack your bags and leave for England immediately! As I am responsible for your being here, I will supply the money for your return fare, and doubtless His Excellency's Secretary will make arrangements for you to be conveyed to the Station."

He paused before he added:

"I have no wish to see you or speak to you again, and when I return home I shall inform your father of your behaviour, which I consider disloyal and a breach of trust."

Odetta did not trust her voice to reply.

She therefore curtseyed and without saying anything left the room.

As she moved away from the door she could hear Lord Walmer still shouting.

Upstairs, Emelene, who had obviously been informed of what had occurred, was waiting.

"Is it true that *M'mselle* Penelope is married?" she asked.

"Yes, Emelene, and she is very happy."

"You know His Lordship is very angry?"

"Yes, I know," Odetta replied drily, "but Mr. Johnson has inherited a large Estate and has come into quite a lot of money."

"*C'est bon!*" Emelene exclaimed. "I think love in a cottage would be very uncomfortable."

Odetta laughed as if she could not help it. Then she said:

"As I am in disgrace, I have to leave here immediately, so I must pack, Emelene. I am sorry I cannot alter any more gowns for you."

"You have been *très gentille*," Emelene said. "Already I have sold the blue gown for quite a good sum. Now I give you a gown for yourself, *M'mselle*. Which would you like?"

"Do you really mean that?" Odetta asked.

"But of course! It is only right after you have worked so hard," Emelene insisted.

It was difficult to choose, but finally Odetta selected a pretty day-gown in deep blue with a small coatee that matched it.

It was elaborately trimmed with braid, but otherwise it was much more simple than Lady Walmer's other gowns, and Odetta knew it would be far more practical for her than anything else, however pretty, which she would be unlikely to wear.

She had thought for a moment that she should take the silver gown as a memento.

Then she told herself it would only make her unhappy to be reminded that the Earl had thought she looked like a star in it and she had been wearing it when he kissed her.

Emelene also gave her the hat that Lady Walmer had worn with the gown, and although Odetta felt it was far too smart for her ever to wear it, she nevertheless accepted it gratefully.

"When you get home, Emelene," she said, "if you will bring the gowns I have not had time to alter down to the Vicarage, because you know I shall never be allowed to come to the Hall again, I will work on them."

Emelene threw up her hands with delight. Then she most condescendingly helped Odetta with her packing.

It did not take very long, although as Penelope had suggested she included the new Worth dresses she had left behind.

While Odetta was fastening the last trunk, a servant came upstairs to say that Mr. Malet had ordered the carriage for her to take her to the Station at five o'clock and wished to see her before she left.

Odetta guessed this was to give her the money for her fare, and she wished she were rich enough to refuse.

However, she knew she could not afford to do so, and having said good-bye to Emelene she went downstairs to Mr. Malet's office, which he shared with Mr. Sheffield.

"I have bought you a First-Class ticket, Miss Charlwood," Mr. Malet said, "otherwise I think you might find it a little uncomfortable travelling alone."

He spoke in rather an embarrassed manner before he added:

"I did suggest to His Lordship that I should send a Courier with you, but he refused to entertain the idea."

"I will be all right," Odetta answered, "but it was kind of you to think of it."

"I have, however, sent a Courier to the Station," Mr. Malet said, "to see to your luggage and put you in a compartment which will be occupied only by ladies."

"Thank you," Odetta murmured.

"There is nothing more I can do," he went on, "and when you reach Calais, ask for a cabin on the Steamer, and on the boat-train find yourself another compartment from which men are barred."

Odetta was aware that he was genuinely concerned about a young girl travelling such a long way alone, and she knew that if her father were aware of it, he too would be worried.

But she knew that Lord Walmer in his rage only wanted to be rid of her as soon as possible, and there would be no point in her saying she felt nervous and was unused to travelling.

Only when the train steamed out from the Gare du Nord and the Courier, a pleasant little man, had waved good-bye, did she feel rather lost and forlorn.

Then as she sat back in a corner-seat she thought that she was after all Cinderella.

If the Earl knew what had happened, he would realise that her carriage had become a pumpkin and the gown she was wearing, which she had made herself, was, if not rags, shabby and out-of-date and very unlike the silver gauze in which he had last seen her.

She gave a little sigh.

'The stars have gone out,' she thought, and felt the tears come into her eyes.

*   *   *

Odetta spent an uncomfortable night as the train did not reach Calais until six o'clock in the morning.

Then she thought it was somehow in keeping with her feeling of unhappiness that it was raining.

There was a mist over the sea, and the passengers alighting from the train shivered as they stepped out onto the wet platform.

However, there were plenty of porters, although the one who carried Odetta's luggage looked at her disparagingly. She knew he was thinking he would not get a very large *pourboire* from a woman who was travelling alone and who was not at all smartly dressed.

He did not hurry himself to get her aboard the Steamer, and when finally she followed the other passengers pushing their way aggressively up the gang-plank, it was to find it impossible to book a cabin because they had all been taken.

The reason for this was very obvious when the ship sailed: it had been waiting for another train to arrive before it did so.

There had been a storm the night before, and the sea was still choppy with a decided swell once they were out of the harbour.

However, Odetta knew she was a good sailor, because her father and mother had often taken her to Yarmouth in the summer, and it had amused her father to go out fishing in small boats which would pitch and toss unpleasantly.

Because she had never felt sick and had in fact enjoyed the days that were rough rather than those that were smooth, Odetta was aware that while she was fortunate, most people would succumb easily to *mal de mer*.

Therefore, she was determined not to go down into the crowded cabin where the passengers, while not actually being sick, sat with white faces, groaning with every movement of the ship.

She found a seat that was sheltered from the rain, and

sat down, thinking once again that she was leaving the Earl behind in France and wondering what he had felt when he had waited for her the previous evening and she had not come.

Had he been anxious that he might never see her again, or merely indifferent?

It was difficult to be certain what he felt, and she kept asking herself whether he had really known the same rapture as she had when he had kissed her and she felt as if the doors of Heaven had opened and she had passed through them.

She tortured herself with thinking that to the Earl she was just a flirtatious married woman who was prepared to be unfaithful to her husband and to let a man she had only met twice kiss her in such an intimate manner.

He might not have felt it, but to her it had been a wonder beyond words, a glory and a rapture that she knew was indelibly engraved on her heart and she would remember it to her dying day.

"I love him!" she said with a little sob.

They must have been well in sight of the English coast when a man sat down on the seat beside her and started to talk.

"Are you travelling alone?" he asked. "It's surely something a pretty young lady like yourself shouldn't be doing!"

Odetta looked at him in surprise, coming back from one of her day-dreams with a jerk.

The man who had spoken to her was obviously a rather common, flashy-looking individual, perhaps a commercial traveller.

For a moment she did not answer, and he went on:

"Now don't be uppity with me. I'm only trying to be friendly. It's a lonely job, I can tell you, crossing and re-crossing from England to France, and I never could make friends with them 'Froggies.' "

The man laughed before he continued:

"Not that their women ain't a bit of orlright. Very dashing, some of 'em are, and not only in looks."

He gave her a leering glance and said:

"But I always say it's the English for me every time, and you're a regular English daisy if I ever saw one, and very much to me taste!"

Odetta tried to snub him by ignoring him, but he would not go away.

He talked on and on, and it was a relief when the boat reached the harbour and everybody began to gather up their hand-luggage.

"Now, if you're going to London," said the man, who had told her his name was Dail Danvers, "I'll look after you an' find you a comfortable seat with me."

"There is no necessity," Odetta said coldly. "I wish to travel in a coach for ladies only."

"Go on!" Mr. Danvers exclaimed. "That'd be a waste of a journey, and no mistake! You and me can have a proper talk together and enjoy ourselves—why not?"

He gave her a nudge before he added:

"Toss an English penny and it'll turn up 'heads' every time!"

The gang-plank was put into place and Odetta picked up the case that was lying on the deck at her feet.

As she did so, Mr. Danvers, who had risen, put his arm round her waist.

"Now, come on, dearie," he said, "stop looking down that pretty little nose of yours! There's no need for me to tell you what I intend to have, and what I intend to get!"

As he spoke, for the first time Odetta felt frightened by him.

"Go away and leave me alone!" she said fiercely.

He merely laughed and tried to pull her closer to him.

There was an expression in his eyes that frightened

her, and she thought too late that she ought to have left him ages ago and gone down into the Saloon, however unpleasant it might have been.

As they struggled, a cabin-door behind them opened and a man stepped out.

Because she was struggling so hard with the persistent Mr. Danvers, Odetta did not see him, and, as she fought herself free, she fell against him.

She put up her hands to steady herself, and as she did so she raised her head and felt as if time stood still, and she was definitely dreaming.

For looking down at her, an incredulous expression in his eyes, was the Earl!

Chapter Six

If Odetta was surprised, no less was the Earl.

He stared at her in sheer astonishment before he exclaimed:

"Odetta! What are you doing here?"

It was impossible for her to reply, and after a moment he said:

"You got my note? I sent one with a footman to the place where we had arranged to meet."

"N-note?"

Odetta's lips seemed unable to form the words, but the Earl said:

"I explained that my grandmother had died and I had to return to England immediately, but I do not understand . . ."

Before he could say any more, there was a commotion all round them. The Steamer having docked, the porters had come aboard and were looking for customers.

"Porter, Sir? Porter?"

One of them pushed himself between the Earl and Odetta, and at that moment she realised that she was not dreaming and the Earl was actually there.

With an inarticulate little murmur she turned and ran away from him along the deck and down the first companionway she came to.

She pushed her way past those who were climbing upwards, weaving in and out of them so that several people complained irritably as she crossed their path.

She did not hear their voices. She had only one idea in her head, and that was to escape from the Earl so that she would not have to explain her presence on board.

Only as she reached a lower deck did she realise that that was where her luggage was, and she saw her own cases standing by a mountainous pile of other trunks. She hurried towards them.

"Porter, Ma'am?"

There was a porter beside her.

"Yes, yes," Odetta answered. "Please collect my baggage. I have to get ashore immediately!"

The porter, who was young and active, obeyed her before any of the other passengers searching amongst the pile for their own belongings were ready. He led the way across the lower gang-plank and onto the Quay.

Odetta did not look up in case the Earl was leaning over the top-deck rail, searching for her, although she thought it was unlikely.

"I have to catch a train for London," she said to the porter.

"Th' boat-train, Ma'am?"

"Is there another?"

"Yus, Ma'am, but it's a slow 'un an' stops at every Station."

"Get me a seat on that one," Odetta ordered.

The porter did not question her decision. He merely pushed his truck to another platform and found a compartment which was labelled: LADIES ONLY.

Odetta sat down in the seat that was farthest from the

platform, hoping that if the Earl did look for her, she would not be noticed.

She was sure anyway that he would travel on the boat-train and expect her to be on it too. But she did not feel safe until, with a great letting off of steam, the train moved slowly out of the Station after the boat-train had already left.

Then with a deep sigh, as if she let all the breath out of her body, she leant back and closed her eyes.

She had seen him! She had seen him again, but she had been too much of a coward to tell him why she was there.

How could she explain? How could she possibly make him aware that everything she had ever said to him had been a lie?

She was not French, not a *Princesse*, not a married woman, but only a dreamer and a liar.

At the same time, she wanted to cry because, even more vividly than she had realised it last night and earlier today, she knew she had lost him.

It somehow made it worse that he would now think of her not as someone so beautifully dressed that he thought she had come down from the Heavens, but instead as a shabby individual struggling with a common man.

She realised now that Dail Danvers had vanished quickly when a Gentleman appeared.

She supposed he was the sort of bounder who would prey on defenceless, unattached women but would be very much a coward if they had masculine protection against his impertinence.

But he was unimportant. What mattered was that the Earl had seen her as she was, and Odetta was well aware that the clothes she was wearing would be indicative of her true position in life.

'I have even been sacked from the position in which I

was employed!' she thought wryly, and felt that that was the last humiliation.

The porter had been right. The train was a very slow one, stopping every few miles, so that Odetta did not reach London until very late in the evening.

When she changed Stations, she found, as she had feared, that there would be no train to carry her to Lincolnshire until very early the following morning.

She was far too frightened to look for an Hotel and thought, although she was not certain, that no respectable place would accommodate a young woman travelling alone.

She therefore sat in the Ladies' Waiting-Room for the rest of the night, and because presumably it was not an unusual occurrence for it to be occupied after dark, nobody enquired why she was there.

She slept a little, but most of the time she sat thinking of the Earl, feeling as if he haunted her so completely that he was there beside her, his dark blue eyes looking into hers, his lips slightly twisted in one of his cynical smiles.

Even to think of him made her love seem to well up inside her like a flood-tide.

She knew that when he had kissed her he had taken her whole heart into his keeping and it would never be hers again.

*   *   *

When dawn came and there was movement on the platform, Odetta made enquiries and discovered that there was an early train which she could catch, although there was no First-Class carriage attached to it.

With difficulty she found a porter to assist her with her luggage, and when finally the train started off, she realised it was going to be a long time before she finally reached home.

In fact, it was very late in the afternoon when she finally arrived, to be faced with the difficulty of getting from Bourne to Edenham.

As she was worrying over the quite considerable expense of hiring a carriage of some sort, she fortunately saw one of the farmers whom she knew.

She hailed him, and as she expected he obligingly offered her a lift.

He was an old countryman, in a very different category from Simon Johnson and his family.

He made her as comfortable as he could and talked slowly of country affairs all the way to the village.

He did not seem to notice that she did not answer him, and when she thanked him for his kindness in bringing her home, he merely said:

"It be an unexpected pleasure an' privilege, Miss, t' 'ave a talk wi' ye. Remember Oi t' th' Vicar."

"I will do that," Odetta answered, "and thank you again."

When Hannah opened the door, she was very surprised to see who was standing there.

"I wasn't expecting you, Miss Odetta!" she exclaimed. "I heard from someone up at the Hall only yesterday they'd no word of His Lordship coming home."

"I will tell you all about it later, Hannah," Odetta replied, "but for the moment I am very tired."

"You look done in," Hannah exclaimed, "and you're a mess if ever I saw one! Whatever have you been doing to your gown?"

"Sleeping in it!" Odetta replied.

She ignored Hannah's cry of horror and went into the Study to find her father.

As she expected, he was writing industriously at his desk, which was piled high with books.

"I am back, Papa!" she exclaimed.

For a moment she thought that he looked at her as if

he could not come back from Greece, or wherever his thoughts were, to recognise her, then he said:

"Odetta! My dear child! I am glad you have returned. I have missed you."

"Have you really, Papa?"

"Yes, of course! It has been very quiet without you here. Did you enjoy yourself in Paris?"

"It was very nice," Odetta replied.

It was an inadequate word with which to describe all that had happened and everything she had felt.

For the moment she could not speak of it, although she knew she would have a great many explanations to make once it was known that Penelope and Simon Johnson were married.

Of one thing she was determined—she would not speak of the Earl to anyone, not even to Hannah.

*   *   *

The next day Odetta slept late, then felt too listless to make the effort to do anything.

It was when Hannah started to unpack for her that the questions came quick and fast.

There was not only the new gown that Emelene had given her, which had Hannah exclaiming in astonishment, there was also the surprise of finding Penelope's gowns in her luggage.

"Why have you brought Miss Penelope's gowns here?" she asked. "And why did you come back alone? I suppose you left Her Ladyship in London?"

"No, she is still in Paris," Odetta said weakly.

Hannah put down the gown she was examining in the light from the window.

"Are you telling me, Miss Odetta," she asked, "that you travelled alone all the way from Paris?"

"It is a long story," Odetta replied, "and I am too tired to talk about it now."

"His Lordship allowed you to travel all that way unaccompanied? It's a scandal—that's what it is!" Hannah protested. "I shall speak to your father about it."

"No, no, please, Hannah! Do not do anything like that. If you want the truth, His Lordship dismissed me because he was so angry."

"Angry?" Hannah queried. "Why should he be angry with you, I'd like to know?"

"I expect you will hear the reason sooner or later," Odetta said. "Miss Penelope has married Simon Johnson!"

For a moment Hannah just stared at her. Then she said:

"So it's true, then, what folks have been saying—that Miss Penelope's been meeting young Simon in the woods. I never believed it myself."

"It is true," Odetta said, "and they are very happy."

"Bless my soul!" Hannah exclaimed. "That's a surprise if ever there was one! And I suppose His Lordship was so incensed that he sent you packing for allowing it to happen."

Odetta smiled because Hannah was so quick on the uptake.

"That is the story 'in a nut-shell,' " she said. "So I will not be going to the Hall again, and I expect someday Mrs. Simon Johnson will be coming to fetch her pretty gowns."

Hannah's attention was back on the new fashions.

"Let's pray she doesn't turn up until we've had time to copy them!" she said fervently.

Because she could not help it, Odetta laughed.

*   *   *

The next few days seemed to pass very slowly.

Odetta learnt from Hannah that the village was in a turmoil of excitement over Penelope's marriage, but there was no sign of Lord and Lady Walmer. And nobody knew what Squire Johnson's feelings were on the subject of his new daughter-in-law.

Odetta longed to have a letter from Penelope, but she thought it was too much to expect, and anyway Penelope would not know that she had returned home.

Everything seemed somehow unreal, and Odetta felt as if she moved through the days like a zombie and lived only at night, when she could shut her eyes and think of the Earl.

Then once again she was in his arms and he was kissing her beside the cascade in the Bois.

Because she loved him so much, she felt as though there was a stone in her breast which grew heavier day by day, and it was hard to feel or to think of anything else.

"I love him! I love him!" she said a thousand times, and was sure it was something she would go on saying until she died.

A week after she had returned home, a letter arrived at breakfast-time addressed to her father, and because as usual he was engrossed in a book, he set it on one side and made no effort to open it.

Because Odetta was mildly curious, she said:

"Do open your letter, Papa. It might be a royalty from your Publishers."

She thought it was unlikely, but it was the one way to make him interested in his correspondence.

She could always be sure of his attention by mentioning books, while other matters appertaining to the village, the Church Services, or the world outside Edenham left him cold.

"It is more likely to be a bill," her father replied with a flicker of humour. "You open it, dearest. I just want to make sure I get this reference down while it is still in my mind."

Odetta picked up the letter, noted that the envelope was made of a thick and expensive parchment, and slit it open with the silver butter-knife.

Then as she drew out the letter she saw that it carried an impressive crest at the top.

"This is from Oxford, Papa," she said.

He did not reply, and she knew he had not heard her, so she read the letter through and gave a sudden cry.

It was so loud that her father raised his head.

"Listen, Papa, listen!" she cried. "This is very exciting! In fact, it is the most exciting thing that has ever happened to you!"

"What is it?" her father asked indifferently.

"I told you this letter was from Oxford, and it is to tell you that you have won the nomination for a Grant."

"What are you saying? What are you talking about?" the Vicar asked.

Odetta got up from the table and walked to his side to hand him the letter. Then she leant over him as he read it.

It was, as she had said, very exciting.

Her father was informed that among other Grants made by Christ Church, which had been his College at Oxford, was one which was extended to Scholars who were researching ancient religions and cultures, and his book *The Influence of the Vedas on Civilisation* had been selected as the most worthy of further research.

The awarders had voted unanimously that he should have a Grant of five hundred pounds a year so that he could continue with his writing.

As the awards were being distributed at the end of the Trinity, the Dean of Christ Church looked forward to entertaining him as his guest on the fourteenth of June.

"That is a week's time," Odetta said. "Oh, Papa, how thrilling! You do understand? This means that we are rich!"

"It is a very great honour," the Vicar said in a low voice.

He read the letter through again, as if he could not believe what Odetta had told him.

"My Publishers must have submitted my book without my knowledge," he said, "and I had no idea that they were even thinking of doing so."

"It is wonderful! Wonderful!" Odetta cried. "Think what a difference it will make! We can have so many luxuries we have never been able to afford before . . . a woman from the village to help Hannah, and perhaps . . ."

Odetta stopped.

She had been about to say: "Perhaps I could have some new clothes," until she realised that her father was not listening.

He was just staring at the letter he held in his hand, and she knew he was thinking only of his book and that someone appreciated it, and he was not in the least concerned with the material advantages which the Grant would bring him.

Later, Odetta realised she would have missed something of importance if she had not looked into the envelope again.

There was a slip of paper asking three questions: First, if the Vicar wished to accept the Grant; second, if he would accept the invitation to stay at Christ Church; and third, if he wished to bring his wife, son, or daughter with him to Oxford.

Odetta wrote in reply to all these questions. Then, when her father was content to sit in his Study rereading his book that had won the award, she faced the eternal problem of what she should wear.

Fortunately, she had the day-gown complete with the little coat and hat that Emelene had given her, but she was well aware that she would need an evening-gown, and those she had worn with the Earl had been left behind in Paris.

It struck her that if she had known her father was going to have so much extra money, she might have asked Emelene if she could buy one from her. But it was too late now, and Hannah said:

"You can't go dining in Oxford with all those Dons and such-like in the gowns you have now."

"I do not suppose they are very smart," Odetta answered with a smile. "They are more concerned with people's brains than with their bodies."

"If you don't have a decent dress, it's over my dead body!" Hannah said firmly. "We'll go to Bourne and buy some good material for a change and copy one of those gowns that belong to Miss Penelope."

Hannah was so enthusiastic about her idea that it was difficult for Odetta not to respond.

At the same time, she could not help feeling that it did not matter what she wore.

If every man in Oxford was an Adonis, she knew they would mean nothing to her, and their faces would merely be a blank because none of them was the man she really wanted to see.

Hannah of course had her way, and they set off for Bourne, with Snowball between the shafts of the cart in which the Vicar, when he remembered to do so, visited the Parish.

Although it took them a long time, they finally reached the market-place.

There were the usual farmers' wives there, selling country fare, and quite a number of them smiled and nodded both to Odetta and to Hannah. But today they had no time to gossip.

The largest Haberdashers was the one for which in 1848 Charles Worth had made the Easter bonnets, the sale of which had enabled him to reach London.

Odetta had always thought they must have been very

beautiful, decorated with lace and artificial flowers as was the fashion in that year.

They had also been very large and very unlike the elegant little bonnets that surmounted Worth's creations today or his rakish hats which had caused a sensation when worn first by his wife Marie.

That was six years ago, when hats with brims were considered extremely masculine.

Odetta had been told that when Marie Worth had appeared wearing a hat with a brim, in the eyes of some people in Paris it was akin to a woman wearing trousers, so much did it smack of dashing masculinity.

"No lady should ever make herself conspicuous!" had been the rule laid down by the stricter elements of society.

But the Princess von Metternich, always in the forefront of a new idea, had no such qualms, and when Marie Worth drove round Paris in a hat with a jaunty brim, she followed.

Odetta and Hannah had no sooner entered the Haberdashers than the Proprietor and his assistants surrounded them.

"You have been in Paris, Miss Charlwood!" they cried. "Did you see Charles Frederick Worth? If you did not see him, you must have heard of him."

"I saw him and I talked to him," Odetta replied.

There was a shriek of excitement at this. Then she was plied with questions, with everyone talking at once.

What did he look like? Was he the success everybody said he was? Did he really fit the Empress when she ordered his gowns? Was it true that the fashions had changed since last year? Were crinolines really finished?

Odetta answered every question as best she could, until Hannah with her usual sound common sense said finally:

"Now, we've no time for more. We need some of your

best dress material for an evening-gown. Miss Charlwood's
going to Oxford."

"To Oxford, Miss? Why should you be going there?"

Then of course the story of the Vicar's recognition as a
scholar was told, and Odetta knew with satisfaction that
it would be all over the town within the next hour.

She was thrilled for her father because she had thought
for a long time that few people appreciated him, and all
too often he was laughed at behind his back because he
was absent-minded.

Now they would know how clever he was, and she
thought it sad that her mother, who would have been so
delighted, was not alive.

But there was little time for regrets. In fact, there was
no time to do anything but sew for the next few days.

The only material in Bourne that looked expensive
and pretty enough was pale blue satin.

It was so near to the colour she had worn at the Masked
Ball that Odetta's first impulse was to refuse to buy it.

Then she knew not only that it was impossible to explain to Hannah why she did not wish to wear it, but also
there was little or no other choice.

The Haberdasher could find no tulle in exactly the same
colour. But there were some ribbons in a deeper blue
edged with silver, and Hannah decided those would deco-
rate the satin in the same way that Charles Worth had
used long ribbons on one of Penelope's gowns.

Then, at the last moment, just as they were leaving,
the Proprietor found not tulle but some soft net in very
much the same shade, which both he and Hannah decided would make attractive flounces round the hem of
the skirt and encircling the neckline.

Again Odetta wanted to refuse, but anything she had
to say was swept aside by Hannah, who drove back in
triumph, clutching their purchases on her lap as if they

were too precious to be set down on the floor of the cart.

Penelope's gowns were more complicated than they appeared, but somehow Hannah and Odetta managed to copy the great swirl at the back, the tightness of the bodice, and the small sleeves that seemed almost like wings as they fell from the low shoulders.

When she first put it on and saw her reflection in the mirror, Odetta felt like crying out that it was an agony beyond anything she could bear to see herself as she had been that night when a sarcastic voice had asked:

"Have you just dropped down from the sky to amuse us poor mortals?"

She could see the faintly mocking smile on his lips, the breadth of his shoulders, and she thought she could feel again the vibrations that came from him.

She remembered how they had waltzed together under the stars; remembered too, almost as if it were still happening, how they had sat for a long time over supper and he had said:

"*Princesse* Odetta is a lovely name for a very lovely person."

That was what he had thought then, because she was wearing the blue gown.

But the last time he had seen her she had not been a *Princesse* but herself, and she was sure he was now thinking that he had had a lucky escape in not becoming involved with anyone so insignificant.

However, the new blue gown once again transformed her, and even Hannah was impressed.

"It certainly does something for you!" she said. "That man has talent, I'll say that for him."

Odetta came out of her dreams of the Earl to laugh.

"If they heard you talk like that in Paris, I think they would lock you up in the Bastille!" she said. "They worship Worth. They think he is more important than the Emperor!"

"I don't believe it!" Hannah said stoutly. "After all, he was only a boy from Bourne."

"He is not even a man now, for they think of him as a kind of god!" Odetta teased. "In fact, a Journalist wrote that 'in Paris the men believe in the Bourse and the women believe in Worth'!"

"Then they should have something better to think about," Hannah said tartly. "Clothes are all right in their proper place, I'm not saying they're not, but there's other things in life besides dolling yourself up."

Odetta laughed again as Hannah always amused her. But when she took off the blue gown and hung it up in the wardrobe, she had a feeling that in some strange way she had recaptured a tiny part of the dream that she had left behind in Paris.

There was a tremendous commotion in getting her father from Edenham to Oxford, for there were not only Odetta's clothes to worry about but also his.

The Vicar fortunately could still wear the frock-coat in which he had been married, although it was slightly out-of-fashion. But it was well-cut, and when Hannah had sponged and pressed it he looked very smart.

"All this fuss," he kept saying. "If you ask me, I had better stay at home and work on my book. The sooner I have it finished, the better."

At the same time, Odetta knew that he was in fact gratified by the congratulations he had received from all his Parishioners and by the fact that the work to which he had given his whole heart and soul was being acclaimed by those who were qualified to judge.

Odetta was more practical than her father when it came to the handling of money. She knew what a difference five hundred pounds a year would make to them, and with this addition to the Vicar's stipend, small though it was, she felt as if they had suddenly become rich.

"When I come back from Oxford," she said to Hannah,

"we will buy some new covers for the sofa and chairs in the Drawing-Room, and certainly a new carpet for the stairs."

"Now don't you go throwing your money about, Miss Odetta!" Hannah warned. "I'm not saying we don't need a number of things, but it's wise to spend slowly and think twice before you do so."

"There is one thing I am not going to think twice about, Hannah," Odetta replied, "and that is your wages. Mama used to feel ashamed that we gave you so little, and now you shall have double what you are having already, besides a present for you to put on one side and save for your old age."

"Do I have a say in whether I have it or not?" Hannah asked.

"No," Odetta answered, "but Papa and I will give it to you with our love and you will take it because you love us."

She kissed Hannah as she spoke, and she knew there were tears in her eyes.

The day before she left for Oxford, Odetta received a letter from Penelope, which began:

I do not know whether You are home yet, but this is just to tell You how happy I am, and how wonderful it is to be with Simon. I have not heard from Papa, but I am sure He is very angry with Me!

Perhaps one day He will understand that nothing matters except the happiness I have found with my Husband.

Please write and tell Me what He and Step-Mama are saying and doing and remember that I am always grateful to You, dearest Odetta, because You helped Me to be brave enough to marry Simon when He came to Paris.

The letter ended in child-like fashion with a number of kisses, and Odetta thought with a smile that Penelope had never grown up and perhaps that was why Simon was so fond of her.

Not being over-intelligent himself, she thought perceptively, he would have been frightened of a sophisticated, sharp-brained young woman who would probably have found fault with him.

As it was, Penelope would think him wonderful and they would undoubtedly live happily ever afterwards.

It was a fairy-story after her own heart, and when she thought of them it was impossible not to feel a little pang of envy.

Her own fairy-story would not have a happy ending, and just as her gown was imitation Worth, so for the rest of her life she would have to make do with imitation happiness.

But how, she asked herself, could she ever find even a faint imitation of the rapture, the ecstasy, and the wonder that the Earl had given her when he kissed her?

She could still feel as if the moonlight on the cascade had entered into them both to make them glow with a strange, flickering flame of fire that moved through her body and from her lips into his.

Merely to think of him was a joy and an agony combined, and yet it was still only a memory and not the real thing.

As her father read all the time on the train to Oxford, Odetta had a chance to sit and think.

Then at last she saw what had been called "The City of Spires" with its fine old Colleges and the streets crowded with undergraduates.

It was different from any place she had ever seen before, and she thought in its own way it was as beautiful as Paris.

She was awe-struck by the huge Quadrangle of Christ Church, and when they were received by the Dean and a number of Dons, she knew that for the first time in her life she was seeing her father against the background to which his intelligence and his learning entitled him.

Because she had been so preoccupied in thinking of the Earl, she had not realised how good-looking her father was.

But now, being taller than most of the men to whom he was talking, he seemed to stand out not only as an intellectual but as a man.

The Dean told her that her father was to stay in the College, which delighted him, but she was to stay with him and his wife in their private house.

"There will be a dinner-party in your father's honour this evening, Miss Charlwood," the Dean said, "to which I am afraid you will not be invited, as it is entirely a masculine affair. But tomorrow you will be able to be present when your father receives his award, and in the meantime my wife and I will do our best to entertain you."

"You are very kind," Odetta answered. "I feel it is a very great privilege to be here."

She spoke formally. Then she added impulsively:

"And I am so very, very glad for Papa!"

"So am I," the Dean replied. "I am a great admirer of your father, and I was hoping this book would be chosen to win the Grant. It is outstanding in every way."

Odetta thought it was so marvellous to hear her father acclaimed with such sincerity that she could not help being amused when, on her arrival at the Dean's house, his wife said the moment they were alone:

"I can see you are wearing the very latest fashion, Miss Charlwood. Do tell me where you bought anything so attractive."

"I have been in Paris," Odetta explained.

The Dean's wife clasped her hands together.

"You are not telling me you are wearing a Worth creation? It certainly looks like one, and I cannot tell you how much I have wanted to see one for myself."

Just for a moment Odetta was tempted to make her happy. She had the idea that the gown with the short coat, which Lady Walmer had bought in Bond Street and which Odetta had altered, was actually one of Worth's designs.

Then she told herself firmly that never, never again would she lie.

She would tell the truth, however difficult it might be, however much it cost her, and perhaps in some little way it would help her to expiate the sin of lying to the Earl.

"I am afraid," she said quietly, "that this is only an imitation of *Monsieur* Worth's design as introduced to Paris. While the gown I shall wear tomorrow evening is almost an identical copy of one of his very beautiful and very expensive evening-gowns."

As she spoke, she saw the disappointment in the eyes of the Dean's wife.

But somehow she felt a little happier in herself because she had resisted the temptation to lie.

Chapter Seven

Odetta spent the next day with the Dean's wife going round the Colleges and meeting a great number of people, all of whom praised her father and said how interesting they thought his book was.

Some had read some of his earlier Treatises that he had written on the same theme.

"You do see that we do not forget our great men," the Dean's wife said with a smile.

This was after several of the Christ Church Dons had told Odetta how they had been at the University at the same time as her father and were so delighted to have him back with them again.

"The next thing we must do is to invite him to join us," one of the Dons said. "Would you enjoy living at Oxford, Miss Charlwood?"

"I think it would be delightful!" Odetta replied.

"I know a great many young men here who would think the same," the elderly Don said, "but I am not sure it would help them to concentrate on their work."

Those who were listening laughed, and Odetta felt a little shy.

At the same time, she wished that her mother were here, and she knew how thrilled she would have been at the chance of leaving Edenham, which she had always felt restricted her husband and was a waste of his intellect.

When her father came to the Dean's house before dinner, Odetta realised he was so elated that he looked younger and happier than he had since her mother had died.

Because she wanted him to be proud of her, she had taken a great deal of trouble in arranging her hair in the same way that she had worn it in Paris.

When she put on the blue gown at which she and Hannah had worked so arduously, she felt as if time had rolled back and once again she was daringly setting out for the Masked Ball.

But tonight the mask was missing, and so was the Earl. As she looked in the mirror, she saw not herself but him with his red-lined Venetian cape flowing back over his shoulders and a faintly mocking twist to his lips.

'I love him!' she thought despondently. 'But what is the point of continuing to say so?'

Downstairs, the Dean's wife exclaimed at the beauty of her gown and the elegant way it was swept back in a fashion she had never seen before.

"I feel dowdy in my crinoline," she said. "The first thing I shall do when you have left is to go to London and find a gown that looks like yours."

"I am sure the crinoline will soon be discarded altogether," Odetta said. "When Mr. Worth sets a fashion, the whole world follows it."

"That is true," the Dean's wife agreed, "but it is very expensive for our poor husbands!"

Everybody had a glass of champagne at the Dean's house. Then they walked across the lawns which sloped down to the stream and entered the College by the Dean's private door.

They walked from the Quadrangle into the Great Hall, where both dinner and the ceremony of awarding her father the Grant was to take place.

"This is an innovation of our own tonight," the Dean explained. "Because the Grant is financed by a generous Christ Church man for a past member of Christ Church, we have invited a number of those who were up at the same time as your father."

"I only hope I have not grown too senile to recognise them," the Vicar said with a smile.

This remark made Odetta look at him a little anxiously, for she was well aware how absent-minded he was, and she knew that when he was concentrating on the past he would often forget the names of his Parishioners.

Tonight, however, he appeared to be enjoying himself so much that his thoughts were very much in the present, and she felt everything would go well.

They reached the Senior Common Room where they were to gather before the dinner, and as they went through the door she realised that there were a large number of men already present and looked quickly at her father's face to see if he recognised them.

Then she heard the Dean say:

"First, Charlwood, I must introduce you to a benefactor of the College and the donor of your Grant—the Earl of Houghton!"

Odetta felt she must have misunderstood what the Dean had said.

Then, when she saw who was standing beside him, her heart seemed to turn several somersaults and she felt almost dizzy with the shock.

It was the Earl, looking just as he had looked the night she had dined alone with him, magnificent in his evening-clothes and seeming to be taller and more outstanding than any other man in the room.

Their eyes met and she knew that he was as astonished

as she was. Then he was shaking her father's hand and saying how delighted he was that he had been the winner of the Grant.

"Now you must meet his daughter," the Dean interposed, "Miss Odetta Charlwood!"

With an effort Odetta remembered to curtsey. She could not look again into the Earl's eyes, but when he touched her hand she felt as if the vibrations that came from him joined with hers and they were as close as they had been when he had kissed her beside the cascade in the Bois.

Then it was impossible even to think of anything except that he was there or to understand what was being said to her.

At dinner she somehow conversed with a charming and intelligent Don who sat on her left, and she managed to reply to the questions which the Dean asked her about their life at Edenham.

But all the time she was conscious only of the Earl, who appeared to be completely at his ease, laughing and talking in a manner which told her he was enjoying himself.

What did he feel about her? What did he think? Was he angry because she had deceived him? And worse still, did he feel nothing but contempt for her lies and subterfuge?

It seemed as if the dinner, which was delicious, went on interminably.

At any other time she would have enjoyed the beauty of the candle-lit tables, ornamented with the ancient silver which was part of the treasures of Christ Church, and the unique experience of being one of the few women amongst a crowd of men.

But somehow it all seemed unreal, and only when her father rose to speak after he had formally been presented with the Grant did she force herself to listen to him attentively.

She knew by the way he spoke how happy and gratified

he was, and when he had finished, the Earl rose to his feet.

Odetta clasped her hands together because his voice seemed to vibrate through her and aroused strange emotions which were difficult to control.

He said he had permission from the Dean to reveal the secret which until now had been kept from their distinguished prize-winner.

It was that he was to be offered a special Fellowship which would be vacant that Autumn, as Professor of Theological Studies at Christ Church, and this he hoped the Reverend Charlwood would accept.

This, Odetta realised, was what everybody had been hinting at all day, but she had never thought it would actually happen.

She could imagine nothing that would give her father greater pleasure and also relieve him of the chores of being a Parish Priest, which he had long found interfered with his academic work.

She looked at him as the Earl spoke, and felt by the expression in his face that he was a man who had unexpectedly found the El Dorado he had always sought.

'How happy this would have made Mama,' she thought to herself, and then she felt that wherever she was, her mother would know.

When dinner was over, Odetta found that the Dean and his wife had invited all the guests to join them on the lawn at their house for coffee and liqueurs.

It was a lovely evening with the sun sinking in a blaze of glory behind the spires and towers of the city, and there was a translucence in the sky in which the first evening star was just beginning to appear.

Odetta walked across the soft grass of the lawn, conscious that the train of her blue gown rustled silkily behind her and also aware that the man to whom she was talking was paying her compliments, although they did not seem to reach her mind.

When the cigars were lit and her father was surrounded by a crowd of old friends, reminiscing of the days when they were young, she felt a firm hand under her arm and knew she was being drawn away towards the stream.

She felt her heart begin to beat frantically, but she did not dare to look at the man beside her, and they walked quietly without speaking until they reached the bank and even then they went on walking.

Only when they were out of sight of those on the lawn did the Earl come to a standstill and take his hand from Odetta's arm.

She felt as if she had reached the seat of judgement and she felt herself tremble as she realised she was facing the Earl and he was looking down at her.

After a moment, as if his silence was intolerable, she said in a very small voice:

"I . . . I am . . . sorry."

"Why did you run away?"

It was not the question she would have expected him to ask first, and she had been trying to think how she could explain to him why she had lied at the Masked Ball. After a pause she replied:

"I . . . I thought you would be . . . angry with me."

"I am very angry!"

"I am . . . sorry . . . I . . . I did not mean to . . . I-lie. I was . . . pretending that I had been . . . asked to the Ball . . . and I therefore had to be . . . somebody . . . other than . . . myself."

"I am angry because you ran away in that ridiculous fashion on the boat," the Earl said. "I thought you must have gone ahead of me to the train. Then when I reached London you were not there, and I could not imagine how I could ever find you again."

"You . . . you wanted to . . . f-find me?"

"Of course I wanted to find you!" he said sharply.

"But . . . I was . . . not the . . . person you . . . thought I . . . was," Odetta said a little incoherently.

"You mean you were not the *Princesse?*" he enquired.

Although she did not look at him, she thought he was smiling as he went on:

"I knew that already."

"How . . . could you have . . . known?"

"For one thing, I was aware that you were not French, even though your accent was quite convincing."

Odetta gave a little quiver, and when she did not speak the Earl went on:

"But that was immaterial, because that night at the cascade I knew you were the star for which I had always searched and by the mercy of God I had found and could hold in my arms."

What he said and the deep note in his voice as he spoke made Odetta blush. Then she said:

"But . . . I . . . was . . . acting a l-lie and I am . . . ashamed."

"Are you ashamed that I kissed you?" the Earl asked.

"No . . . no!" Odetta replied quickly, without thinking. "Only that I . . . should have . . . deceived you."

"You deceived me about nothing that mattered," the Earl said firmly. "What was wrong and wicked and drove me almost insane was that you disappeared from the Steamer and I had no idea how I could see you again."

Because his voice was now accusing, Odetta said nervously:

"Forgive me . . . please . . . forgive me."

As she spoke she raised her eyes for the first time to his, and then it was impossible to look away.

His arms went round her and slowly, very slowly, as if he was savouring the moment, he pulled her close to him.

Looking down at her, his eyes gazing into hers as if he searched for her very soul, he said:

"I will forgive you only if you promise never to vanish again into the Heavens or anywhere else."

"How . . . could I?" Odetta murmured.

"It would be impossible," the Earl said, "for I will never let you leave me!"

Then his lips came down on hers and swept away her fear, her unhappiness, and everything except the rapture of knowing that this was what she had been longing for and thought she had lost forever.

He kissed her while time stood still and yet she felt as she had at the cascade in the Bois, that he carried her up into the sky and they were one with the stars and no longer human but Divine.

Only when finally he raised his head and she was trembling with ecstasy and sensations she had never felt before did she stammer incoherently:

"I . . . love . . . you! I . . . love . . . you!"

"That is what I wanted you to say," the Earl said, "but I thought I would never find you to hear you do so."

As if hurt by the thought of what he had felt, he pulled her almost roughly against him.

Then he was kissing her again, fiercely, passionately, demandingly, in a way he had never kissed her before.

She was not afraid, but there was a fire within him which she felt burned its way through his lips and into hers, and she felt her whole being respond in a strange manner that was still part of the rapture and the stars.

The Earl held her even closer and she could feel his heart beating wildly in unison with hers.

Then at last the intensity of it was too much, and with an inarticulate little murmur she moved and hid her face against him.

For a moment it was impossible for him to speak, until

with his lips against her hair he said in a voice which
seemed strange and a little unsteady:

"How can you make me feel like this? I believed I
should never fall in love, and yet it has happened, and I
still can hardly credit that it is true."

"I . . . told you," Odetta whispered, "that . . . it was
the . . . magic of . . . Paris."

"And now perhaps you will say it is just the magic of
Oxford, but the magic, my precious one, is in you and is
something I will never lose, because I could not live
without it!"

The way he spoke made her raise her face to look
at him, and she saw there was a smile on his lips which
was not mocking as he said very quietly:

"How quickly can we be married?"

It was then that Odetta felt as if she were waking from
a dream as she had when she had seen him on the Steamer and was aware of how dowdy and insignificant she looked.

Without even thinking, she said the first words that
came into her head.

"B-but you . . . cannot m-marry . . . me."

"Why not?"

"Because I am not . . . what you thought . . . not even
as I . . . appear tonight."

"You look very beautiful," he said quietly, "in the same
gown in which I first thought you were some celestial being."

Odetta made a sound that was half a choked laugh and
half a sob.

"It is . . . not the same. It is an . . . imitation, and that
is . . . what I . . . am!"

She saw that he did not understand, and she went on:

"I went to Paris in the . . . position of . . . lady's-maid
to my friend . . . Penelope Walmer, who was staying at
the British Embassy. As I was only the . . . daughter of
the local Vicar . . . I was not . . . allowed to take . . .
part in their . . . social activities."

She spoke quickly because she felt she must tell him the truth, and her words fell over one another as she went on:

"I had altered some gowns which did not . . . belong to me, but because they were so . . . beautiful . . . I wore one of them and . . . pretended to be . . . somebody who was . . . entitled to wear . . . them."

As she spoke she felt that she was throwing away her chance of happiness and the Earl would be aware of how contemptible she was.

But his arms were still round her, and she said brokenly so that he could barely hear:

"When you saw me . . . on the Steamer, struggling with that . . . vulgar man, I was myself . . . dowdy . . .insignificant . . . a nobody!"

As the last word died away she hid her face once again against his shoulder, and now there were tears in her eyes and she was trembling.

It struck her that she had been extremely stupid in telling him the truth, but everything about the Earl was so noble that she knew she could not lie or go on trying to deceive him.

Because she loved him, she had to be honest and straight-forward, even if it meant she lost him.

For a moment he did not speak, and she felt an agony that was physical sweep through her body, and she wanted to cry out at the pain of it.

Then he said quietly:

"My ridiculous darling! Do you think I love you because of what you wore or what you pretended to be? I love you because you are you, because from the moment I saw you my heart told me I had found something I had been seeking all my life!"

Odetta gave a deep sigh.

She did not dare look up at him as she asked in a whisper:

"Is . . .is that . . . true?"

"Very true, as I shall prove to you," he said. "Long before I kissed you I knew that fate had meant us for each other, and we were joined by a magic that was not of this world but came, if you like, from the stars to which you belong."

"How can you . . . say such things?" Odetta asked. "How can you . . . even think . . . them?"

"They are true, my darling one, and I defy you or anybody else to tell me that we do not belong to each other and you are not already a part of me that is indivisible."

Then as Odetta stared at him, speechless, he was kissing her again, but this time she felt that his lips were compelling and demanding, as if he would not allow her to refuse anything he asked of her and there was in fact no escape.

Only when she was trembling not with fear but with a rapture that pulsated through her did he say:

"Now answer my question. How soon will you marry me?"

"You are . . . sure . . . absolutely sure that you . . . really want . . . me?"

"It will take me a long time to make you sure," he answered, "perhaps a century, so the sooner we start, the better!"

He was smiling as he spoke and his voice was very gentle, yet she thought there was a note of love in it that she had never heard before.

"I am not . . . important . . . enough."

"You are the most important person in the world to me," the Earl corrected, "and I am the one who matters!"

"Then . . . please," Odetta said, "I want to marry you . . . and it would be the most wonderful . . . the most perfect thing that could ever . . . happen."

The Earl would have kissed her again, but she put up her hands to stop him as she said:

"Supposing . . . just supposing after we are . . . married, you are . . . disappointed and . . . ashamed of me?"

"I shall not be disappointed," he said firmly, "and I promise you I shall be very proud of anybody so beautiful and, because you are your father's daughter, so intelligent."

Odetta gave a little sigh, then it was impossible to speak because the Earl's lips were on hers.

It seemed a long time later before she stirred in his arms and said:

"We must go back . . . but please . . . you will not tell anybody tonight about . . . us?"

"No, of course not," he answered. "This is your father's night of glory, and we must not take it from him."

"That is what I wanted you to think . . . and it is so . . . wonderful that you do!"

He smiled, and she knew he was thinking that they thought the same things.

"It seems impossible," she said, " that I have hated you as Mama did for so many years."

"Hated me?" the Earl repeated in astonishment. "But why? And how did you know of me?"

Odetta gave a little cry.

"I forgot . . . I forgot that I have not told you . . . who Mama was."

"We have not had very much time for conversation," the Earl said wryly, "since you ceased to be a French *Princesse* and came to Oxford with one of the most brilliant men Christ Church ever produced."

Odetta gave a little laugh as if she could not help it.

"Mama's name was Houghton."

"Houghton!" the Earl exclaimed. "Are you saying she was a relative of mine?"

"A very, very distant one."

"But why should she and you have hated me?"

Odetta drew in her breath.

"About eight years ago Mama wrote to you asking i
you had a living you could offer to Papa."

The Earl stiffened.

"I remember!" he said. "Good God! I remember! An
I refused."

"You said you would follow your father's advice an
not do any favours for . . . relatives, who always . .
complained."

"I remember," the Earl said. "I remember writin
that letter."

He put his arms round Odetta and said quickly:

"You will have to forgive me. You have no need to b
ashamed, but I have. It was because of the many prob
lems relatives had caused my father that I felt like that.

"Papa never knew Mama had written to you, but sh
was very . . . hurt, and when . . . you told me your nam
in Paris, I wanted to . . . hurt you."

"Instead you hurt yourself," the Earl said perceptive
ly. "But, my precious, again fate has taken a hand, an
quite inadvertently I think I have made it up to you
father."

"Why did you give him the Grant?"

"I read his book and I thought it absolutely brilliant
Then I told the Dean I would like to give the Grant fo
any man who had been at Christ Church and could writ
like that. I had a number of other books sent to me t
read, none of which in any way reached your father
standard of originality and intelligence."

Odetta gave a little cry of joy and the Earl continued

"But I will explain more fully why I wrote that lette
My father had been plagued by two relatives who ar
fortunately dead now; on one of them he spent an enor

mous amount of money which was lost gaming and in riotous living, and the other was a cousin who attempted to blackmail him."

"How horrible!" Odetta murmured.

"It made him very angry," the Earl said, "and because he told me what had happened, it made me for the time suspicious of all my relatives, especially when they kept asking me for favours once I had inherited the title."

"I can understand now," Odetta said, "but it was only because Mama felt that Papa was wasting his brains at Edenham that she was brave enough to write to you."

"I can never forgive myself for being so negligent as not to make some enquiries about your father at the time," the Earl said, "but perhaps you will forgive me when I tell you that it was my idea that a special Fellowship should be created for him at Christ Church, and I have in fact contributed a certain amount of the Endowment towards it."

"Oh, thank you, thank you!" Odetta cried. "It is wonderful! How can I tell you how happy this makes me?"

"By marrying me very, very quickly!" the Earl answered. "It will only complicate things if your father assumes that you will be living with him when he comes to Oxford."

"I do not . . . think that you are really . . . considering Papa, but . . . yourself!"

"I am being entirely and completely selfish," the Earl agreed, "but I want you! I want you now, this moment, and for eternity, and I do not intent to wait!"

There was a determined note in his voice and an authoritative air about him that made her smile.

Then, because she was so happy, she put up her arms to pull his head down to hers as she said:

"I will . . . try to make you . . . happy. I love you, and it has been an . . . agony I cannot . . . describe to think I would . . . never see you . . . again."

"How could you do anything so wicked?" the Earl asked. "If you suffered agonies, so did I, and it is something I intend never to go through again!"

He kissed her as he had before, passionately, demandingly, and almost as if he punished her for what he had suffered.

Then he said:

"Tomorrow when you leave here you will come with me to Houghton Rex. I want to show you our future home, and I intend that your father will marry us in my Private Chapel."

"When . . . do you want to be . . . married?"

"The day after tomorrow, or at the latest the day after that," the Earl replied.

For a moment the wonder of it seemed to Odetta to envelop them with a light that came from Heaven.

Then she gave a cry that was very human.

"B-but I cannot . . . I cannot marry you . . . so quickly . . . I have . . . nothing to wear!"

The Earl laughed.

"That is a very feminine remark."

"But I . . . want you to . . . admire me and think I look . . . pretty . . . but how can you when I have only two gowns, this one and the one I shall wear tomorrow?"

The Earl laughed again.

"My precious darling! You have been listening to those ridiculous women in Paris who think and talk of nothing but their clothes. I will adore you in anything you wear— and in nothing!"

Odetta blushed and he smiled before he said:

"I never did believe there was a *Prince* hiding in the background."

"I . . . wore a . . . wedding-ring."

"I will give you a real one."

Odetta's eyes were sparkling and the Earl went on:

"You shall also, my darling, have all the gowns you

want from London. Then I suggest, if it will make you happy, we will start our honeymoon in Paris and I will buy everything you require from the inestimable Worth."

For a moment Odetta contemplated what it would mean if Charles Worth should design her gowns, in which she knew she would look glamorous and bewitching and certainly lovelier than she had ever looked in her life before.

Then she looked up at the Earl, his head now silhouetted against the stars filling the evening sky, and she said:

"It will be very . . . exciting, but it does not really . . . matter. Nothing matters except that you . . . love me and will go on . . . loving me as I love . . . you."

"You may be sure of that," the Earl answered. "I love you, my precious, and nothing—not even the gowns which you think so important—matters. We belong to each other, our hearts, our minds, our souls are one, and very soon our bodies will be one, too."

There was a solemn note in his voice and Odetta could see the love in his eyes and she felt as if there was a light glowing in them to which her own responded.

It was so perfect, so wonderful, so part of everything that she believed was sacred and part of God, that she whispered passionately:

"I . . . love you . . . but I am afraid I am dreaming, and I shall . . . wake up to find this is . . . just another of my . . . fairy-stories."

The Earl laughed and it was a very tender sound.

"Dreams do come true, my lovely one," he said, "and this one is true from now until the stars fall from the sky and the world comes to an end."

Then he was kissing her, kissing her until Odetta knew that once again he was carrying her up into the sky, and there were stars in their eyes, on their lips, and in their souls.

It was not a dream, but reality.

ABOUT THE AUTHOR

BARBARA CARTLAND, the world's most famous romantic novelist, who is also an historian, playwright, lecturer, political speaker and television personality, has now written over 200 books.

She has also had many historical works published and has written four autobiographies as well as the biographies of her mother and that of her brother Ronald Cartland, who was the first Member of Parliament to be killed in the last war. This book has a preface by Sir Winston Churchill.

Barbara Cartland has sold 100 million books over the world, more than half of these in the U.S.A. She broke the world record in 1975 by writing twenty books, and her own record in 1976 with twenty-one. In addition, her album of love songs has just been published, sung with the Royal Philharmonic Orchestra.

In private life, Barbara Cartland, who is a Dame of the Order of St. John of Jerusalem, has fought for better conditions and salaries for Midwives and Nurses. As President of the Royal College of Midwives (Hertfordshire Branch), she has been invested with the first Badge of Office ever given in Great Britain which was subscribed to by the Midwives themselves. She has also championed the cause for old people and founded the first Romany Gypsy Camp in the world.

Barbara Cartland is deeply interested in Vitamin Therapy and is President of the British National Association for Health.

Barbara Cartland's NEW Magazine

Barbara Cartland's
World of Romance

If you love Barbara Cartland books, you'll feel the same way about her new magazine. *Barbara Cartland's World of Romance* is the new monthly that contains an illustrated Cartland novel, the story behind the story, Barbara's personal message to readers, and many other fascinating and colorful features.

You can save $4.73 with an introductory 9-month subscription. Pay only $8.77 for 9 issues—a $13.50 value.

So take advantage of this special offer and subscribe today using the handy coupon below. <u>For less than 98¢ an issue, you can receive nine months of the best in romantic fiction.</u>

SUBSCRIPTION ORDER FORM

Yes, I want to subscribe to *Barbara Cartland's World of Romance*. I have enclosed $8.77 (check or money order), the special introductory price for nine issues of the best in romantic fiction. (Canadian subscribers add $1.00, $9.77 for nine issues.)

Name_____

Address_____

City_____State_____Zip_____

Send to: Barbara Cartland's World of Romance
57 West 57th Street
New York, N.Y. 10019

NO RISK: If you don't like your first copy for any reason, cancel your subscription and keep the first issue FREE. Your money will be refunded in full.

This offer expires September 1981.

BC-4

Barbara Cartland

The world's bestselling author of romantic fiction. Her stories are always captivating tales of intrigue, adventure and love.

☐	12273	THE TREASURE IS LOVE	$1.50
☐	12785	LIGHT OF THE MOON	$1.50
☐	13035	LOVE CLIMBS IN	$1.50
☐	13830	THE DAWN OF LOVE	$1.75
☐	14504	THE KISS OF LIFE	$1.75
☐	14503	THE LIONESS AND THE LILY	$1.75
☐	13942	LUCIFER AND THE ANGEL	$1.75
☐	14084	OLA AND THE SEA~WOLF	$1.75
☐	14133	THE PRUDE AND THE PRODIGAL	$1.75
☐	13032	PRIDE AND THE POOR PRINCESS	$1.75
☐	13984	LOVE FOR SALE	$1.75
☐	14248	THE GODDESS AND THE GAIETY GIRL	$1.75
☐	14360	SIGNPOST TO LOVE	$1.75

Buy them at your local bookstore or use this handy coupon: